Stuff: A Novel

STUFF: A NOVEL. Copyright © 2024 by Audrey Wright

ISBN: 978-1-304-20444-8

Stuff: A Novel

Audrey Wright

Dedication:

To my husband, Eric, there with me and for me through every outlandish endeavor. The stuff of our lives is the stuff of my dreams.

To my kids, Sam, Norah, and Eli, for inspiring me to be my best self. You are at the center of all I do. It is for you. Always for you.

To my parents, for showing me that there are many ways to exist in the world, and they are all worthy of celebration.

To my brother, Nate, the songwriter, who uses words to create beauty every day, and who reminds me that creating things is a noble calling.

To my girlfriends, who know me and still have unconditionally supported me all my life.

To my students at The Park, for trusting me to let us become writers together. Your success is my capstone.

Chapter 1

"For what are your possessions but things you keep and guard for fear you may need them tomorrow?... And what is fear of need but need itself?... Is not dread of thirst when your well is full, the thirst that is unquenchable?"

- Kahlil Gibran *The Prophet*

The tall thirty-something woman in front of Beth in the checkout line set a bottle of Merlot, a bag of pork rinds, and a pregnancy test on the conveyor belt. While Beth stared, the woman shuffled through her purse for her I.D. As the cashier typed in 1992 to validate the alcohol purchase, Beth wondered what kind of night the woman was having. She shuddered. Was the wine to celebrate a minus sign and the pork rinds to mourn a plus sign? Or vice versa? It was hard to tell as the woman took the brown paper bag -- her long, manicured fingers gripped around the bottle's neck -- and stalked off.

Beth reached up and rubbed her neck, curling her fingers around her collar to loosen its grip. She smiled politely at the cashier, a young man who couldn't have been twenty

1

years old. He started to pick up her items, scan them without interest. Her basket *was* less interesting. Gummy vitamins, two bags of frozen vegetables, and five Lean Cuisine meals for one.

"Is that all?" he mumbled, raising his eyebrows.

"No, just these couple things," Beth said, distracted by the impulse purchases beside her in the "candy-free" aisle. She grabbed a VW Beetle Matchbox car, an emery board and clipper combo set, and a pack of two claw-shaped hair clips in a tortoise-shell pattern. She hated hair clips but loved tortoises. The cashier rolled his eyes, scanned her items, asked if she wanted cash back.

"No, thank you."

She looked down, watched her sandal as she drew a circle in the spilled cereal on the floor.

"Receipt in the bag?"

"Sure." She hurried outside, fleeing a judgement no one had bothered to make.

*   *   *

No one had ever had reason to pity her. She was lovely, always had everything *just so.* Her auburn hair was never out of place and was always sleek, even on Michigan summer days when the humidity was higher than the temperature and there was never enough sunscreen to stop the freckles. She was fit, too; every day she ran for miles, craving and abhorring the solitude as she breathed deeply, crossing ice, mud, steamy pavement, or crisp leaves. Every outfit she put on, fit. She accentuated her ensembles with all the right accessories, particularly the latest designer handbag, always large and chic and occupied by her chihuahua, Goliath. He was her constant companion, strong through every difficult day.

Today, however, was not one. Today she had a coffee date with the accounting guy at work. *Chris*, she thought, *was cute, available, and probably good with money.* He had been asking her for a while, but she kept refusing. She couldn't decide if she was disinterested, pessimistic, or playing hard to get. So last week when they were serendipitously together in the cafeteria line and he asked again, she relented.

Now, she started her apple-green VW Beetle and drove to the Starbucks closest to work. *Neutral ground*, she thought.

"Beth, hello!" he greeted her from the mosaic-tiled bistro table on the sidewalk-turned-patio. She barely recognized him in his Saturday attire which she privately dubbed, *just this side of slovenly.*

"Hi," she replied and sat in the shade of the awning.

"Grande nonfat soy latte?" he asked, making sure it was still her favorite. She nodded and busied herself with making Goliath comfortable, pulling a small bowl and bottle of water from her bag for him.

He returned with their coffee, and scones she neither ordered, nor ate. Small talk ensued: the weather, work gossip, the Tigers' chances for a win against the Yankees. Never did their words stray from the comfortable and familiar. This was her pattern, two hours of conversation, sixteen ounces of caffeine, but no connection. She couldn't remember later the scent of his cologne; they hadn't even touched.

Thankfully, he'd been so infatuated with her sad smile and faraway eyes that he'd been oblivious to all the things disappearing from the table. A free *Detroit Free Press*, the cardboard sleeve from her cup, and three packets of Sweet and Low made their way unceremoniously into her Chanel handbag next to her dog, the souvenirs of an entirely forgettable afternoon.

*   *   *

Driving home, she punished herself. Maybe she didn't smile coyly enough. Maybe her skirt wasn't properly pressed. Maybe she had lipstick on her teeth. He didn't say he'd call, so the second she got home, she changed into her gardening ensemble and prepared to perfect her front yard. Unlike people, who made her edgy and self-conscious, the garden was within her realm of control. Removing weeds, litter, and deadheading flowers were all tasks she felt competent completing, so she went after them with gusto. She knelt on her gardening cushion to dig up an offending dandelion, then trimmed the grass around her flower border with shears that matched her dandelion digger. As she sat on her front stoop, surveying the lawn, an enormous SUV drove by, back window half-down for child safety. From that window issued a small shoe. It landed in the small area of grass between road and sidewalk, an eyesore of adorable proportions.

Immediately, as he'd been trained, Goliath ran to the shoe, picked it up in his teeth, and carried it through the dog door and into the sunroom that ran across the front of the house while Beth clapped and dug into her apron pocket for a dog treat. He deposited the shoe in the box labeled *front yard litter* and ran back to be rewarded.

It was a small thing that she could have done herself, but it filled her with joy to have a companion equally devoted to perfection. Although she loved the same traits in him that she loathed in herself, she was grateful to have someone with whom to share her burdens.

*   *   *

The small child in the Yukon that drove past Beth's house that day was a nudist. Sure, most babies prefer to go au naturel, but Genevieve was absolutely committed to it. Her prim and proper mother did everything in her power to keep clothes on the child, but from the day she had learned to remove them, it was all over.

Today was the wedding of the child's aunt, a stately affair with red roses adorning every pew and groomsmen in top hats and tails. Even a toddler could see this was a bit oxymoronic for a noon wedding, and Genevieve must have noticed, because as she waited at the back of the sanctuary with her basket of red rose petals, she removed every last stitch of crinoline and lace.

Her soft white skin was much more dramatic against the red carpet than her ruby dress would have been, and her mother fainted away in her seat, rendering herself unable to

6

stop her daughter, who strolled down the aisle, scattering petals and joy.

Therefore, after being stuffed back into that horrid dress, tights, and shoes for pictures and a good scolding, Genevieve decided that she WOULD NOT spend the night dancing in those shoes. So out the Yukon window they went, one into Beth's permanent collection of lawn litter.

*   *   *

As the sun began to set and the mosquitoes came out in vicious numbers, Beth and Goliath retreated to the comfort of the sunroom to watch the sunset. The box labeled front lawn litter was just behind the wall under the windows, out of sight to passers-by who could only see the white wicker furniture and its bright yellow cushions. If they looked closely, they could see large, framed art on the wall -- of daisies to match the furniture. This was the only bit of the inside of the house that could be seen from the sidewalk, because Beth kept the blinds tightly closed at all times. She wrapped Goliath in a yellow blanket as they sat there together, and the sun dipped from view. But they had to go inside sometime.

After a yawn and stretch, Beth decided it was time for bed. She looked out to the street for any sign of people before opening the door and crossing the threshold into her home. The smell of filthy carpet met her nose first, then her eyes tried not to notice the *stuff*. Floor to ceiling, it was piled in boxes, stacked and labeled and covering the entire front living room with only a small path to walk through sideways. It was dark, even with the lights on, and gloomy. She couldn't get to the ceiling fans to clean them, and the blades were thick with dust. Every now and then she considered turning them on, just to see what would happen. The upper corners of the room were filled with cobwebs and the lower corners were a mystery long ago buried by layers of accumulation. Wondering how she'd let it get this bad, she let out a deep sigh, and went to look for the proper boxes for her new acquisitions. Newspapers were in the hall, miscellaneous paper products, such as the cardboard sleeve, were by the back door, and lastly, the Sweet and Low, in a box on the kitchen counter holding free packets of sweeteners of all kinds. While she preferred not to sweeten her coffee or tea except with honey, she may someday have company that would need them, and she would be ready.

Although no one had ever been asked into Beth's house, she spent a lot of time preparing for those future visitors, the ones that she would have over when her life began again. Exhausted, she shimmied through the kitchen into the back family room. It was two steps down, and she had always thought it was a charming touch, like those mid-century rumpus rooms, but now, as she climbed through the bins to the couch that had become her only usable piece of furniture, it seemed that she was descending into an abyss. She begged sleep to come quickly.

Chapter 2

Running is an escape from what must be done, to what can

be done.

As she closed her eyes, sleep wasn't merciful. Away. She wanted to be far away. She could feel the boxes closing in on her like when one too many people got into her office elevator, and she wasn't sure what to do with her hands. In her home, even putting her hands into her pockets was too space-consuming, her elbows sticking out just enough to make her pathways impassable and potentially topple a precarious pile.

In her head, she envisioned a different life, full of open spaces and sunlight, maybe a Costa Rican mountaintop where she could see the ocean over layers of steamy hills, dark then lighter, all the way to the sand. Where cool rain falls on hot brown skin and the air is so thick with oxygen that she can't tell where it ends, and her own body begins. Where she could stand on her head under a grass-roofed yoga palapa as monkeys swung through the rainforest, mocking her as she saw the world from a new angle, tilting it toward enlightenment, a grass mat on the bamboo floor and the cloudless sky glittering above. She would lower herself back to the floor, spend an hour in Savasana, corpse pose. Allow a small death. Encourage a rebirth. That was the dream tonight. Her dream to leave herself behind and begin again - create a retreat where the past and future were not welcome, where there was no room for sentimental pieces of paper or knickknacks, only sky and earth, wind and water, here and now. Why couldn't she be that girl? Why did she court misery, willingly bringing it home like a stray dog, feeling it needed her somehow? When her eyes opened, there were no graceful treetops, no refreshing breezes, no peace, only box after box, a paper fortress she had built to shield herself from the life she really wanted.

It would have been easy to slip back into sleep. She had no one checking on her progress. She could have the day mothers of small children coveted - no alarm clocks, drinking her tea hot, no one commandeering the day's activities, a book in the lawn chair on the patio. In fact, until her Monday morning meeting she would probably not even speak to another human being. She had no one to answer to but herself, and she had already let herself down in more ways than she could count, so when Goliath shook his collar, and his tags chimed their tiny ring, she really had no choice but to get up and get on with it. Sunday was the longest day of the week for Beth. Most people in her neighborhood enjoyed the downtime afforded by a day of rest; they barbecued and lounged around watching baseball on ESPN, or watched their children play in their backyards-- but Beth's Sunday started like every other day--with a solitary run. Goliath's tiny legs couldn't keep up, so he got his own brisk walk around the block in the afternoon.

As he ran around her feet in a tiny circle, rubbing up against bins on all sides, Beth quickly dressed in her running ensemble, carefully curated to avoid blisters, chafing, and visible sweat circles, patted Goliath on the head and headed out into the foggy early morning. She loved to be out a bit before dawn when the sleepy suburb was unaware of her. She felt like she could conquer miles better alone, without the world watching. Every day her feet traversed the same route, avoiding the same potholes and pitfalls. As she ran along, she saw a gorgeous hazy sunrise and got to see the whole neighborhood come alive. People on lawn mowers spreading the sweet smell of fresh-cut grass and dew mingled with smiling children on skateboards and scooters that dodged her as they made their way to their own adventures, and families in their best, backing out of their driveways to church, some singing, some sipping coffee, some grumbling. She blazed past them all on her way to the house that was her midway point and her daily flirtation with joy.

The yard was a disaster. Grass so tall it had seeded, and weeds with uncultivated blooms that would have been the only color had it not been for the toys! Frisbees, pails, tricycles, and bits of water balloons--everything in garish primary colors, haphazardly strewn about. *Just this side of slovenly.*

For years her daily visits to this house at the end of a not-terribly-interesting cul-du-sac had been met with the expectation that someday it would be neat--that someone might look out through the dirty windows and be appalled that the world could see their mess, their lack of order. Lately though, she turned onto that street with a feeling of dread, worried that it *would* be neat. Worried that the family who lived there would not have a house surrounded by peals of laughter, off-key singing, and weeds, but rather surrounded by a moat of calm and joyless order.

As she rounded the corner into the loop that would send her back home, she found her dread unfounded. The closely clipped lawns along the block helped to ease her mind. They contrasted so obviously with the house her eyes were searching for. Toys were barely visible today; the grass had gotten so tall.

As she usually did, Beth slowed her pace a bit and checked her heart rate at this half-way point in her run. She could have done it anywhere, but she wanted to give herself the best chance to catch any sound she could from behind the chipping paint on the once-white windowsills. Straining to listen, she was caught off-guard by the bike rider that flew down the driveway from behind the garage with a handlebar in one hand and a golf club in the other.

"Fore!" the rider yelled as an old volleyball skidded across the sidewalk just in front of Beth's sneakers.

Beth stopped abruptly as the bike followed closely after the ball. Over her shoulder, the little girl who looked to be about seven years old, brown braids whipping back, continued by adding, "Sorry! I watched polo on T.V. last night, and we don't have a barn for horses, so I'm using my bike. Have you ever played polo?" Beth had continued down the sidewalk and the little girl trailed after her, golf club still in hand. "Well, have you?"

"No, I haven't. I don't know that many Americans have."

"I'm gonna add pro-*fesh*-uh-nul polo player to my bucket list. Do you have a bucket list?"

More like a list of buckets, Beth thought cynically, but responded with, "I think we all do, informally."

"I keep mine in an orange bucket from Home Depot, but it's almost full. Mom says I need another bucket."

"I think I saw a blue one in your yard a couple days ago. You could use that."

"Oooo, really? Gotta look. Bye! Have fun running!"

And she was gone. The rear tire of the bike was still spinning as it lay on its side in the sidewalk. She could faintly see the grass moving but suspected that the girl was making a trail on her hands and knees through the tall grass in search of a blue bucket she could fill with still more huge plans.

As she turned and ran out of the cul-du-sac toward her neighborhood, she ran slower. There was no rush to hide herself away for fear of being known. After all she knew what awaited her beyond the perfect lawn lined with an explosion of purple and yellow annuals, the cheerful porch, the barrier of dusty blinds. She could see the sentimental towers on either side of her, stretching forward farther than her imagination would allow. There were countless buckets, but she'd forgotten how to dream.

*   *   *

Or maybe she hadn't. She could just leave. Goodness knows she spent a great deal of her childhood planning and attempting escapes.

One morning in third grade, she packed her backpack full of necessities: granola bars, five Barbie dolls with several ensembles each, a pack of Crayola markers, and a set of plastic teacups. She wasn't exactly sure where she would go, but she knew that her house was no longer her favorite place. It wasn't the warm and cozy place she remembered with bedtime stories and tea parties. Instead, it was full of angry stares and wordless dinners where the silverware clanked too loudly on the china plates. She wanted a place to go where she could control how everyone behaved, and she would make them love each other. That evening her father found her huddled in a thicket on the edge of the playground behind her school, a granola bar wrapper caught in the thorns above her head. She hugged him tightly, her little legs wrapped around his waist. It wouldn't be the last time he would have to prove he would come find her. She was eight. She couldn't fix things. But she could run away.

Didn't she leave it all behind every morning on her run, albeit too briefly?

As she sat on her front steps, hair still wet from her shower, Beth pondered where to run *to*. Chicago was a great city - so many sights to see. She had fond memories of the Ferris wheel at Navy Pier and loved to run along the lakeshore and watch the waves. Traverse City had the lake too, plus wineries and street fairs, and all those little boutiques full of summer must-haves. She didn't have any bedazzled flip flops for this season yet. Both places were a little far for a quick weekend getaway though, and Goliath hated long car rides. *Wait, yesterday Chris had mentioned a quaint little town just an hour north*, one with little downtown shops full of antique teacups, trails through the countryside, and the open spaces she so craved. He had talked about the authentic Victorian B & Bs it had. *Had that been a missed invitation?*

She went inside and googled the Chamber of Commerce and found the perfect bed and breakfast and then saw the announcement that made up her mind - that the very next weekend was the village-wide garage sale. Oh, how she loved garage sales, yard sales, rummage sales and all the glorious and inexpensive stuff she could buy: truly treasure. The best part was that those things that people displayed out in their driveways on card tables, the litter of their lives, were full of memories of lives lived, but the memories weren't hers.

They could be seen but didn't have to be felt. Like buying a pair of jeans at the Salvation Army, already beautifully broken in. Oddly, Beth didn't find it difficult to be nostalgic about a past she didn't remember. Instead, she found it freeing; to carry someone else's baggage was somehow lighter.

Just then her thoughts were interrupted by Goliath leaping from the top step and chasing a rogue leaf across the yard. As the wind picked it up and sent it twirling through the air, Goliath ran in a roundabout pattern, tracking it like a hunter and snatched it down with a little growl as if to say, "You've been conquered. Accept defeat." He strutted back to the porch, where the front yard litter container was awaiting its next acquisition. The bright yellow leaf fell into the shiny red shoe like some random still life painted to hold on to youth and beauty. As if they could be held.

Chapter 3

The soul can be revealed by showing the world what we

choose to keep.

To leave as much room as she could for the bargains she was sure to find, Beth packed light. It took a while to find her box labeled "Fourth of July," but all holiday bins were kept in the spare bedroom so that narrowed it down. She did have to climb over the dusty exercise bike *who bikes inside?* and because summer was nearly over, it was underneath the Fall holiday bins, but two sailor blue and red outfits would be perfect for whatever Labor Day festivities were happening. There was sure to be a parade, so she brought a small American flag on a stick and her favorite running shoes, in red. Goliath's essentials were in his bag, and everything fit on the passenger seat. Her floral summer handbag was emptied out in favor of a blue one with metallic stars, and with white sunglasses on top of her head like a headband, Beth was ready to go.

The setting sun poured into her lap making her warm and drowsy. She turned up the music, some pop song with a perky beat, and rolled down the windows sending a swirl of tiny dog hairs up, around, and out the opposite window. Goliath watched them go, head out the window, as if he longed to jump after his lost possessions, but Beth could only think that the car had cleaned itself, and she was grateful. As the highway miles flashed by, the scenery became greener and more open; subdivisions gave way to farms and chain restaurants ceded to mom and pop greasy-spoon diners. With less pavement, it actually seemed to get cooler the farther she went, and she began to feel that this vacation would be the refreshing break she needed.

The B & B was on a quiet street with a steep grade overlooking the town. The house itself had a plaque on the wide veranda wall stating its history back to 1865 and the yellow and lavender paint job stayed true to the town's Victorian style. Beth desperately hoped that she would have the turret bedroom at the house's front corner so she could indulge her princess fantasies and simultaneously keep track of all the neighborhood's yard sale set-up that was sure to occur. In the morning, she would adore the voyeuristic position the windows afforded. She could judge without being judged. There was a *look* to a proper yard sale, and Beth could tell a good one from blocks away. Large furniture pieces were the first clue to quality. It showed her that they weren't just throwing some junk on the driveway because people would be walking by, they had prepared and sought out anything unnecessary.

What would a yard sale look like at my house? What do I find unnecessary? What could I part with? What would I part with? Who would buy my newspapers back to 1992? How could I part with all that news?

The second thing to look for was a rack of hanging clothes. No one wants to dig through piles of clothes that they feel obligated to refold when a stain is discovered. Instead, there's the refreshing sound of hangers sliding across the metal pole and the easy assessment of each item, no folding necessary. Her garage was full of metal poles that would serve as lovely clothing racks, but she couldn't for the life of her think of one article of clothing that she would consider superfluous. Each belt, blouse, pair of socks had been selected for its timelessness. Nope, her carefully crafted wardrobe was not for sale. She could, however, use a green scarf. Beth made a mental note to look for one tomorrow as she crossed the porch and lifted the brass door knocker in the shape of a horse head with a bit in its mouth. Much classier than the doorbell she had at home. The light inside it had gone out years ago, but she hadn't had it fixed. Actually, if there was one superfluous thing on her premises, it was that doorbell.

She let the bit fall. Within seconds, the door was opened by a woman who looked to be in her fifties.

"Hello, I'm Moira. Welcome to my home. You must be Bethany."

"Please, you can call me Beth, and this is Goliath. What a lovely town this is; I've never been before, but so far it lives up to the hype."

"Ooooh, we have hype! How special! I'll have to tell the garden club ladies," Moira crooned with an earnest smile lighting up her face. "Can I take your things up to your room?"

Beth instinctively backed away from this request and said she hadn't brought much but would love to be shown her room. "Is it the lovely front turret bedroom? Please say it is!"

"Well, of course, my dear! You may have any of the three available rooms... Business isn't what I'd like these days. No nostalgia."

The staircase was the centerpiece of the house and had a beautiful curve to it, perfect for Christmas garland, wedding pictures, or a child to slide down when no one was watching.

As they made their way up, Beth paid special attention to the alcoves with shelves built into the walls on the way up, each one housing some small treasure: a bust of a famous author, a lacquered urn, a Hummel figurine. At the top of the stairs was a lovely little sitting area with a bookcase and a knitting basket on a little table between two wing chairs covered in a Delft blue pattern. She longed to explore the house alone, to experience its comfortable clutter at her own pace, but Moira hustled through her home like a woman on a mission, not pausing to dwell on the objects and artifacts that surrounded her.

Beth's room was just to the left of the sitting room and was everything she never knew she always wanted. The four-poster bed dominated the little round room, and from that bed she could see not only the whole street, but also the slanted housetops down the hill all the way to the main street with its storefronts and cobbled pathways, a less exotic version of that Costa Rican mountaintop.

"There is a bathroom in the hall that you will share with one other guest in the opposite bedroom. I hope that's okay."

"No problem; that is what I expected - no en suites in the 1800s," Beth replied and sat down on the edge of the bed, more tired than she expected.

"Or expansive closet space, so feel free to use the bureau. Let me know if there's anything you need. My room is the only one on the first floor. Breakfast is served at eight."

"Thank you so much. Good night."

Beth set her bag on the bed's floral quilt and began to unpack, sliding out the bottom drawer of the dresser with a light squawk. As she was admiring the perfectly empty drawer, she noticed that the bottom of it had been covered with some kind of liner. Upon closer inspection, it was not the normal contact paper, but rather decoupaged newspaper articles. The one that caught her eye had a picture of a young girl in front of an antique store with a young couple standing behind her. A hand-painted sign read, "Whittingham Antiques." Easily mistaken for a business's advertisement, she was surprised by the article's headline, "Out of Tragedy, A New (Old) Home." Kneeling, so she could read the smaller print, Beth discovered that the little girl in the photograph had been left next to the dumpster of the antique shop as a baby, and was adopted by its proprietors, a beautiful new life in the midst of beautiful old things. Beth found herself welling up with tears for that little girl and for the mother who found it necessary to discard her.

Too emotional and unwilling to read any of the other articles, Beth covered them with her carefully chosen outfits. On the wooden bench at the foot of the bed, meticulously, she set out her non-holiday outfit for the next day and her running ensemble for the morning. A good three-miler should allow her to scope out the better sales around town and wake up her legs for a day of walking.

As she sat on the side of the claw-foot tub brushing her teeth and ruminating, her thoughts wandered to her own mother and all the times Beth had felt like a piece of furniture in her mother's life. She hadn't been discarded, rather she was a piece of formal living room furniture, stupidly quarantined in a room with impossibly white carpet solely to impress visitors. She had longed to be the ugly recliner in the family room, truly loved.

At five years old, in 1990, Beth had come skipping down the spiral staircase in her favorite sparkly lilac party dress. That night, she was allowed to dance with the grown-ups on the stone patio underneath her bedroom window.

At every previous party, she had watched from above, her button nose pressed against the glass as she breathed in and out so heavily that the window would fog. She drew little hearts in the mist to send down to the dancers, blowing them sweet little vapor kisses.

Waiting patiently for the party to begin, Beth wandered from the kitchen to the dining room and back, dodging the hired servers with their black suits and brisk movements and sneaking an occasional hors d'oeuvres from an untended silver tray. With a canapé in her hand, she backed into the parlor, a room so unfrequented that Beth thought the vacuumed swirling shell pattern in the thick white carpet was part of its original design.

The pointy tips of her mother's stilettos appeared and poked through the doorway; her eyes scanning the room for whomever had committed the crime of making barely visible indentations the size of tiny dancing shoes across her perfect pattern. Was that a crumb? A piece of a Carr's Table Water Cracker, just a few shades darker than tolerable, poking up through the fine threads meant to impress. As soon as those stilettos hit the parlor floor, Beth panicked, shoved the rest of the cracker and cheese into her mouth, and dove further behind the sofa in an effort to delay what she already knew she couldn't avoid. Her mother's manicured finger grabbed her by the back of her lace collar, the polished tip sending a chill as it grazed across the skin over her spine. She was made to stand on the tile of the dining room while her mother took the vacuum from the hall closet and viciously sought to duplicate the housekeeper's accustomed pattern, to turn things back to right.

As Beth watched her presence in the room be erased, her chin began to crinkle, and her bottom lip began to shake.

No guests would use the parlor that evening. No one would notice the subtle change in the angle with which the carpet fibers lay. But Beth would notice every single hairstyle as she watched the grown-ups sway beneath her window until her breath fogged the glass to obscure the scene she had so longed to join. She drew no hearts. She would waste no time creating things that could be wiped away with a towel and some Windex. She would focus on things that last.

Chapter 4

Is there ever anything fashionable enough to cover our

insecurities?

She ran down the front steps and onto the sidewalk, careful to watch for cracks that didn't line up. These sidewalks were full of *character* and on an unfamiliar route there were so many possible dangers: strange dogs, sprinklers, uneven pavement, and too many things to look at. Many of the people were already arranging their things on card tables and using dollies to heft heavy old hutches into their driveways. Thankfully, the sky looked clear. There would be more things displayed on driveways and less in actual garages. This helped avoid confusion about what was for sale and what was merely a garage inhabitant and gave more light for close inspection. She returned to the B&B excited about the day ahead and refreshed by the new scenery. *Back in just enough time to shower before breakfast. What a perfect morning!*

The smell of scones and Moira's smile greeted her. "Welcome back!"

"I was just out for a run!" she said, too loudly. Pulling out her ear bud she asked, "Do you run?"

"Only when chased!" Moira quipped and almost skipped back into the kitchen. There was a warmth in this house. She felt at home here.

*   *   *

Freshly scrubbed and dressed, Beth hopped down the stairs with Goliath on a bedazzled blue leash.

"Well aren't you two fan-cy! Big plans for the day?" Moira glanced up briefly from setting the table with an eclectic collection of china plates and teacups. None of them matched each other, but they all matched the feeling in the room. The quaint flourishes on the table legs and wallpaper, the glimmer of the crystals in the massive chandelier, the intricacy of the patterns in the crocheted tablecloth all spoke of a time when things were not mass-produced. These things had probably been broken, and soiled, and scratched, but instead of being replaced had been lovingly repaired by people who could not bear to part with them.

"Yes! We are going to scour your neighbors' garage sales for hidden treasure! Oh, Goliath, we should have brought our pirate costumes." Beth grinned at her own joke. "What are your plans for today?"

"Well, let's see...I need to weed the front hydrangea beds and clean up the kitchen and polish the silver and finish the last two chapters of my latest romance novel, *Only You!*"

"Are you a writer?"

"Oh no," Moira giggled, more like a schoolgirl than a woman who could have grandchildren in school, "I just love a good love story. The yearly used book sales keep me stocked up. If you had chosen the honeymoon suite, you'd see the shelves are full of them! You know, for inspiration." She winked.

Deciding to change the subject, Beth focused on breakfast. "Do you have any honey for my tea?"

"Of course, dear," and she bustled into the kitchen for an adorable ceramic honeypot and dipper. "I always get local, raw honey. It's supposed to help with allergies and cure all that ails you."

"Nothing is currently ailing me, but you can never be too careful." At that moment, Beth really believed that her statement was true.

They sipped their tea and listened to the song of the bluebird outside the window. It was the most peaceful she could remember being. This trip had already yielded treasure.

But enough was never enough, so she got up and started off on the same path of her morning run. There had been a house down the block with a long metal pole balanced on two stout tree limbs that stretched out over the driveway, and she just knew they would be filled with hangers and clothes by now. Maybe even a green scarf.

The sidewalk was already becoming relatively crowded with other treasure-seekers, so Beth was thankful she'd run so early. It would be impossible, or at least irritating now. Upon reaching the house with the tree-rack, she was delighted with the selection of Depression glass, vintage furniture, and maybe 30 different umbrellas in almost every color, all with very distinctive handles, *probably a collector who had moved on to something new*, but the rack was a definite disappointment. Instead of offering interesting clothes from a bygone era, it contained curtains. There were curtains of lace, brocade, lined, and sheer, all custom-made and very expensive, but useless in a home where windows were shrouded in tightly closed blinds that couldn't be dusted because of the rows of boxes in front of them. They would only add another layer to the darkness in her home. She was looking for anything but that.

So, she pushed onward. The next block had several homes that had just thrown together a couple card tables covered with stuffed animals and snap-suits next to ride-on toys along the edges of the driveway and a random bouncy chair or bath seat. She had heard that children would completely change the amount of time one could spend on her own activities, but this was pathetic.

Then, out of the corner of her eye, Beth saw a bright red and blue slide in the back yard that ended in a kiddie pool that had about three inches of water in the bottom. If she closed her eyes, she could almost manifest the giggles and splashing. She forgot her disgust with the measly sale and lost herself in the joy of a loved child whose mother probably had to fight with herself to part with those stained burp cloths because they represented a time when she was that baby's whole world.

She thought she should stop and look in deference, but she couldn't pillage these mothers' memories. She did, however, resolve to look for a brightly colored bucket for the future polo player on the cul-de-sac back home, goodness knew that she may look forever in that grass without finding one.

Goliath sensed her pause and tugged her out of her reverie and back to the sidewalk.

As she refocused on her search, Goliath was sniffing and being sniffed. A large Rottweiler had taken an interest in him. "Excuse us," Beth apologized to the dog's owner and tugged Goliath's leash, and on they walked after a little canine side-eye.

On the next street up the hill, there was less yard clutter. The houses were better-maintained and shiny cars sat on the curb in front. Beth crossed her fingers and headed toward the first one with a sale. It was a small red two-story with a Juliet balcony in front of open French doors. Border gardens burst with white and scarlet impatiens leading to a weeping cherry tree that had been carefully trimmed so the leaves stopped about two inches from the closely clipped lawn. Half-moon slate steps led to a blindingly white front door. It was perfect.

Beth could not say the same for the organization of the items for sale. They were strewn across the yard with no recognizable pattern. There were five handbags... *handbags!* but they weren't together. What they were, however, was q-u-a-l-i-t-y. A quilted pink leather Kate Spade with a chain handle caught her eye first. She mentally matched it up with three outfits she had at home, but the closure wouldn't allow Goliath to peek out. And there was no price label. Then she saw it. She had missed it because it had blended in with the grass. A square of perfect twill silk with an aristocratic herringbone pattern. *I'd put good money on that being Hermes.* She practically crawled through the grass to it. It was! What a find! *Why don't any of these things have price tags?*

And then it hit her. Not a thought that would make everything clear, not an epiphany about her life and how to fix it, but a shoe. As it turns out, a red, patent leather, four-inch heel, Manolo Blahnik - a la *Sex and the City*. It had the pointiest toe and a sexy curve, and it had hit her hard, square in the forehead, so hard in fact that she ended up face down on that beautiful scarf while she plummeted into unconsciousness and Goliath barked for help.

Chapter 5

If it's all the same to you, give me an old thing, sturdily built, which has had its own life and made its own memories.

Possessing visual clarity that somehow belied her addled mind, she saw steel gray eyes unabashedly staring down into hers with a guilty curiosity.

"So, how did you get caught in the middle of my tantrum?"

She blinked twice. "What?"

She realized she was no longer on the lawn but lying on one of those chic, simple, and modern sofas that appear uncomfortable but felt rather like a feather bed. It was impossibly white, and she immediately worried that no one had removed her not-perfectly-clean shoes. The man, however, did not seem concerned -- about the sofa anyway. "I'm so sorry." He looked at her with a pained expression.

"How much?"

"Excuse me?...Very much! I never would have thrown it if I'd known anyone was out there."

"No, how much did you want for the scarf?"

"Pardon me, but don't you think the lump on your forehead is a bigger concern right now?"

"Not really. I've been looking for just that type of green scarf. I have a work outfit that just will never look completely right without it."

"Well, in that case, it's yours. Not that it makes us even. I intend to pay any medical bills or whatever you need."

"I don't think you need to worry about that. It was my fault for trespassing in your yard and coveting the items in your obviously-not-a-yard sale."

"Yard sale?" With the obtuseness of a man wracked by guilt, he fumbled for her meaning. "Oh! You thought all that stuff was for sale? Oh..."

"Today is the village-wide garage sale. Did that escape your notice as did the woman on your lawn?" she asked, trying to lighten the mood.

He smiled and the corners of his eyes wrinkled softly. Three days of stubble almost obscured the dimple in his lower right cheek, but it did not escape Beth's notice, and she thought to herself that his face was striking and then immediately wondered if hers, no doubt with an enormous red goose-egg and possibly tear-streaked make-up, was as attractive.

"Could I know your name?"

"Of course! It's Adam, Adam Connors. Let me get my insurance information."

"I'm Beth...Bethany," she whispered after him, not sure if he heard. When he returned, she assured him repeatedly that she was fine, the scarf was all she needed, his house was lovely, *his eyes were dreamy, ... wait,* "Where is my dog?"

"We have a little fenced-in area in the backyard. He's back there."

"Thank you so much. I'd be lost without him."

"I find it hard to fathom that you're thanking me when I very nearly beheaded you thirty minutes ago. Really, if there's anything I can do to make up for it, my number and everything is on the paperwork I gave you."

"You have been chivalrous, but I'm really fine. Nothing a long run and a cup of tea won't fix." As she stood up, she was slightly dizzy but soldiered on so as not to add to his already palpable remorse. She gathered Goliath, and they said goodbye.

"Adam, it's been...interesting."

"Likewise. Bethany."

A handsome listener. Irresistible. And yet she walked down those slate steps and out into the Nordstrom-Rack-the-Day-After-Thanksgiving mess of a lawn with a strong stride that showed nothing.

*   *   *

She headed toward town. No eager garage sale sellers, a park bench, anonymity to think. She found an iron bench tucked into a walkway that had probably been a narrow storefront many years ago but had been converted into a cobblestone path and Victorian garden by the downtown preservation society. There was a plaque and everything. It was lovely, dark and verdant, relatively unused by a car-obsessed generation that will drive around endlessly to obtain a parking spot directly in front of the Chinese take-out place.

As she sat, she slid the scarf from her handbag and let the silky tenuity glide through her fingers with the softness of Lake Michigan beach sand. It was so beautiful, so exactly what she was looking for, like the turret bedroom, Moira's honey pot, those gray eyes. Her head was spinning.

Out of the corner of her eye, down the path and across the street, she had a deja vu moment. *Had she been right here, in this very spot, before?* As she stood and turned to her right, the Whittingham Antiques store was directly in front of her.

It was no more vibrant in person than it had been on the faded newsprint, but the patina was not incongruous for a purveyor of the old and lovely.

She had to go in. Compelled by curiosity but also the knowledge that an antique store in a Victorian town would have endless treasures, she moved toward the street, depositing Goliath in her bag and the scarf into her pocket so his tiny claws wouldn't snag it.

The entrance was a heavy, army green, wooden door with copper bells hung to ring when it opened. Looking up, she was surprised to see that they weren't traditional American bells but were on beaded strings and were shaped like upside-down wine glasses and were stamped with designs that reminded her of somewhere exotic, like Marrakesh. If she had a bucket list, Marrakesh was on it.

Crossing the threshold, the smell hit her first. Old books with frayed cloth spines, embossed titles, idyllic stories and a thick layer of dust on top of the gilt-edged pages were lined up on a turquoise bookshelf that she presumed had been built by a hobby carpenter long ago and painted by a housewife looking to bring *a splash of color* into her living room. She almost bought the shelf and all the books in it, when she remembered that she was a long way from home and a Beetle is not really meant for hauling furniture. Beth shook her head in an attempt to shake loose any shoe-inspired impracticality and removed instead a 1942 second edition copy of *The Boxcar Children*. Memories floated around her with the dust as she rested her chin on the top of the spine and blew.

When she had read it as a child, alone on starched linens and surrounded by toys from FAO Schwartz, the children's lives had moved her to tears over her own. She was an only child; they were children. She had a mansion in the city; they had an abandoned boxcar. She especially compared the utensils and cups they found in the dump to her sparkling silver tea set - and found her tea set lacking.

From her balcony, Beth had spent many, many childhood summer nights watching her parents as they entertained their friends and her father's associates. Not really entertaining, not really mingling, but sparkling. In her nightgown, Beth's admiring eyes would stare down through the balusters until her toes tingled with impending numbness. They were so perfect together, so confident. Her mother, Cherisse, was a chameleon, a knowledgeable and cultured woman of the world one moment, and an ornament on her husband's arm the next. She could always summon the persona the situation called for. Real was harder. Motherhood was harder. But Beth didn't blame her. Her mother was everything. If she'd asked Beth to jump, Beth would have responded, "In which shoes?" So as early as five, Beth obeyed when she was instructed to call her mother Cheri, instead of mom. This rule was even more strictly enforced when Beth turned seven, and her parents split up - out of the blue - just before Christmas. The tea set was the first thing she opened that Christmas morning.

Dirty silverware could hold a family together, while polished could tear them apart. When she wanted to take that tea set to Daddy's to celebrate the new year, she was told, "I bought that for you. It stays here. He can buy you a set for his place. Now let's have tea." Bethany put two sugar cubes in her pocket during that tea party.

She cracked her neck, trying to dislodge the memories that were still making her idolize the boxcar children after all these years and roamed through the aisles and displays. Some focused on glassware, others furniture or clothing or tools. After about thirty minutes, she felt drawn to the basement, where there was likely to be more *manly* old stuff. There was a strong odor of mildew as she descended the cement stairs. She barely noticed the rakes and shovels hanging on the walls beside her. And there it was, hanging from a nail pounded into a board holding up the floor above--a tin bucket. It was not bright red, or plastic, but stylistically it was very likely to fit in amid the tall grasses and peeling paint on her favorite cul-de-sac. It was big, too, and the little girl needed lots of room for her dreams. It would hold them securely. The bent metal holding the wooden handle onto the bucket wouldn't snap off like the cheap sandbox play-set handles. *Should she give a gift to a girl to whom she had never been formally introduced?* Somehow, she felt okay about it, even in this world where every day they are finding the bodies of fourteen-year-old girls in the woods, this family was different. They probably wouldn't call the cops on her or question her motives. Probably.

So, she wearily climbed the steps, purchased the bucket and the book from an older woman who gave Beth the handwritten receipt with a hand covered in soft papery brown skin and protruding veins. The words and numbers on the yellowing paper were difficult to read because of the wavy letters. The woman's hand had shaken the whole time, was shaking now, in fact.

"Anne," she nodded toward Beth, "and you are?" Her voice was barely a whisper with a hint of a southern drawl.

"Beth. Thank you, ma'am, for letting me explore your treasures."

"Come again, my dear. It's not often we see customers on garage sale day. Bet it was nice to have the whole place to yourself."

"It was. I'll definitely be back."

And she would be. But not for a bucket. Or a book. But to understand.

*   *   *

As she left the store, a bright light glinted in her eye, but it was only the overhead light reflected in a mirror over an old dresser that had a mint green comb and hairbrush sitting on it. She couldn't imagine ever using someone else's brush and wrinkled her nose and forehead in dissatisfaction at the thought. When she did, a blast of pain shot through her temples, and she leaned forward onto the dresser, making the mirror sway. There was a large red goose-egg halfway between her hairline and her right eyebrow. She felt dizzy and sat in a rattan-seated rocking chair, the kind that when you lean back make you feel as though you are leaning back into the inside of a hamster ball and you try to catch yourself only to realize that the chair is perfect, and you look silly not trusting it. Struggling to place her feet back on the ground without hitting herself in the head with the bucket, she was now even dizzier. Goliath looked up out of his bag. He seemed worried as did Anne, peering over the counter.

"I'm okay, you sweet little pup. Let's go have some tea." She lifted him out, Anne appeared relieved that Beth hadn't been talking to herself, and together Beth and Goliath waved, jingled the bells, and made the uphill trek back to Moira's bed and breakfast. Beth longed for the turret bedroom and to be doted on like a princess. She couldn't see why fairy-tale princesses were always trying to break out of them.

Seated on the iron scroll-work patio chair, trying to balance her teacup on a table without a glass top to flatten it, while balancing a bag of frozen peas on her throbbing forehead, Beth closed her eyes and listened half-heartedly to Moira's rendering of the past few hours. Beth was sure it would take her the same number of hours to tell it as live it, but she was relieved to think about something else, anyone else.

"It hasn't rained in so long that those weeds in my front beds were stubborn, so I worked up quite a sweat after you left. My mother used to say that women don't sweat, they glisten. But *I* sweat. Then I tried polishing the silver, but the heat and the fumes got to me, and I had to sit down. So I did. In the rocker on the side porch. With my book and a cup of tea and this big floppy hat. And you know what? That city girl in the book ended up with the rugged cowboy with a six-pack instead of the dashing city boy with a six-pack!" She slapped her own knee in surprise. "Who would've guessed that abdominal muscles were so vital! I always thought eyes were more important. Gray eyes that pay attention to you, that see right through you if you let them. The city boy had them. Silly heroines anyway..." and just then a breeze blew through the trees that took that hat up and off her damp white curls.

It floated across the yard, like a stingray moving through water, graceful and dangerous, fluttering a little but you'd swear not enough to move that fast. It landed on the side lawn, close to the sidewalk, but it didn't escape the notice of Goliath. He leapt across the green grass, filled with purpose. Snatching the brim in his teeth, he was determined to bring it inside. He tugged and struggled, finally sliding it across the stones of the patio and up to the back door where he whined then barked to be let in. Beth tried to get up quickly, only to sway and catch herself, her hand clutching the side of the table in desperation. Moira hurried to help her, then went and tried to take the hat from Goliath. He wanted to finish his mission and receive his treat, but he couldn't destroy the hat. Destroying things was not permitted. He learned that long ago. So, he let go.

"Helpful little fella, isn't he?!" exclaimed Moira.

"Oh, quite," Beth replied. "I don't know what I'd do without him. For me, it's the only way alone isn't lonely."

"Maybe I should get a dog? Oh, no. Too many allergic visitors. Sometimes this whole making a living really cramps my style."

"I think your style is just right. That hat is perfect, by the way, and keeps your skin like porcelain, I bet."

"An angelic complexion with a halo of soggy hat-hair." She struck a pose. "How's your head?"

"Better. Has the swelling gone down?"

"A little. Let's get you inside and set you up with a good love story. Maybe a princess in a tower?"

"Perfect."

*   *   *

But after Moira left Beth in her turret room, on the complimentary pad of pastel floral paper with a pen shaped like a feather, Beth, not for the first time in her life, wrote a poem titled "Despair." About a man with sad eyes and a roguish dimple who threw things and gave her a beautiful scarf that even as she wore it now gave off a hint of the perfume of a well-heeled wife. She couldn't tell if it was the scent or the dent from the heel that made her head ache. A love story was not what she needed tonight. A good cry would have to be the salve.

*   *   *

Despair

By Bethany Morris

Today is a tidal wave
Of alone.

Kindness, Pain, Beauty, Sorrow

Suffocated by the life I've built in slow piles

Wishing the swell would come and drag it all away

Leaving behind it a swath of emptiness

Lovely destruction

Like a kicked ant hill

That immediately begins to be rebuilt

For a queen that never sees the sun

But I am no one's queen

I collected my misery myself

And today he reminded me that

My misery and myself

May find solace in silk for a moment

But we long to be lifted from the floodwaters

By flesh and bone.

I see a rescuer in the distance

But he is not here to save me

He has his own queen

Hopefully the flotsam of my life

Will float me to shore.

*   *   *

Adam sat at his nook table with a cup of coffee and a real newspaper. He didn't even need to be coerced into a subscription by a grocery store raffle ticket. This newsprint delivery system was best for his psyche. There were no updates, no breaking news bulletins that tickered across the bottom of the screen. Instead, it was all they knew at printing time, all one could take really, he didn't need his tragedy updated minute by minute, but preferred a slow burn.

He read the front-page story about the flooding in Louisiana, then flipped to the sports' section and the Tigers' fight with the Yankees; he'd missed the game but preferred the articulate sports writers' descriptions to ESPN's highlights - yelling and laden with superlatives - trying to make angry men with bats seem like heroes.
Really it was all just a distraction from the destruction in his own house, and the solitary woman who had been its unconscious witness.

He strode through the kitchen, threw the paper in the recycle bin by the door, and went out into the yard to pick up all the things he'd thrown. Dragging his feet through the grass, he sat in the midst of it all and reached over for a silk blouse, lifting it gently, bringing it to his nose slowly to inhale her, before carefully folding what really should be hung. Over the course of the next thirty minutes, he gathered together neatly what had taken him two minutes to scatter, a beautiful pile of expensive women's clothes, the evidence he had tried so hard not to find. She would be home soon, so he deposited it on the table where it would be impossible to ignore, heels on top and minus one scarf.

*   *   *

Asleep on the tabletop, the click of her heels on the entryway tiles woke Adam up to a bewildered evening grogginess. She strode down the hall, the porch light making her body a silhouette through her gauzy sundress. His heart instantly told him to get up, embrace her, love her as he had all these years. Until his eyes fell on the pile of clothes, the pumps he had not bought for her, nor she for herself, and his desire melted into sadness. And then *she* saw them. And the clicking stopped. Her purse slid off her shoulder, and she didn't bother to catch it. It hit the floor, tipped, and spilled lipstick and keys onto the cold white tiles. Her eyes were wide, but her red lips neither smiled nor frowned. Their eyes fluttered from each other to the tabletop and back again. They said nothing and stood so still it was like they were willing time to still itself as well. But who would want this moment to last? *Something else, anything else.*

"Where were you?" Adam asked.

"Out," Dominique replied.

"You've been there a lot lately. Do they have good nachos?"

"The best."

"Why don't you take me with you? I love nachos."

"I don't think you'd like them. They're served with a side of..." She stopped. She couldn't do witty repartee right now. She was exhausted by her day, the conversations she knew were coming, the nagging pit in her stomach. "Can we do this tomorrow?"

"No."

"Okay." She turned back to him and started over to the pantry and fridge. She gathered tortilla chips, shredded cheese, a Tupperware container of day-old taco meat that she hadn't had the first time because she'd been "out," and a jar of black bean and corn salsa. She got two ceramic plates from the cupboard (she'd heard that microwaving plastic was bad) and proceeded to make nachos. *Ding!* She put the nachos on the table and then went for a bottle of Stoli. She made hers with cranberry and his with ice. She brought them to the table, and they both sat down, heavily, wearily.

There are lots of kinds of gray. There's the gray of a cozy cable-knit sweater and the gray of a gathering storm cloud. She was used to the former, but now saw the latter in his eyes. There was a storm brewing. She rethought the choice of beverage a bit too late. Adam was not a drinker. It did not calm his mood, but rather riled it.

"Where did you get all these designer clothes?" he asked bluntly.

"Is it important?" taking a nacho and crunching down on it.

"Is it? I haven't seen any large purchases in the checking, and I looked up those shoes, the Blahnik ones, they are $1000.00 per pair! Do you have some secret credit card or is it something worse?"

A long pause. She had to decide what was most important, his feelings or the truth.

"Stephen," she whispered. His heart fell into his feet, and his head started to spin.

"Your boss? Is this some kind of weird profit-sharing? Help me out here."

"We've been seeing each other for a while. He…cares about me."

"And I don't? What the hell, Dom!"

"You can't…won't… give me the things I need."

"You need shoes? Dresses? What are you, Marie Antoinette? You know how that ended, right?"

"I know it seems shallow, but I…"

"It doesn't *seem* shallow."

"I don't know what to say," Dominique said softly.

"That's because there are no words for this," and he walked away.

Chapter 6

Parades end up where they began, but only the first half

has any cheers.

In the morning, Beth woke to sunshine and the chirping of birds -- wrens -- in a birdhouse hanging from a giant oak limb by her window. There was a late-summer fog lifting and the air was heavy. She had better get out to run quickly, or she may change her mind. She dressed, filled her fanny pack with hydration for Goliath, and made her way down the cracked concrete steps to the street. Her feet felt leaden, but she forced herself to keep moving forward. She passed a cemetery, saw massive stones from long ago, *BELOVED WIFE AND MOTHER, TAKEN TOO SOON,* and more modest, recent markers with fresh flowers and closely trimmed grass. It looked like a peaceful place, with its rolling hills, drooping boughs, and empty benches. She decided to run through, might as well get some hill-training while she was at it. At the top of the hill, she saw a small but ornate headstone with the name Whittingham. On the left, it said John 1932-1999. On the right, it said Anne 1939-   . Anne was 78 years old and had been a widow for 18 years. She wondered who was lonelier, herself or Anne. They both had pets, although cats and dogs were generally like apples and oranges in terms of affection, but to have known a partner's devotion for so long, was the lack of it like an unfillable void? Did they love each other until death did them part? Was it a relief to try a different life? Was there even room in her own life for anything else? Unanswerable questions filled many of her runs, but today she wasn't sure she needed more questions. She would prefer answers.

She headed for the street with Adam and his house with the red door. There was a silver Ford Taurus in the driveway that hadn't been there yesterday, and the designer lawn art was gone, as was the Jeep Wrangler that had been parked in the spot now occupied by the Taurus. She ran past, hoping to avoid meeting whomever else lived there, great taste in clothes or not. She was sure they would never be friends, even if they had more in common than just a silk scarf.

Down the hill she went, right to Main Street with its quaint shops and barber poles mixed with the incongruous neighbors of sushi restaurant and head shop, the modern small town. As she perused the town, she noticed empty blankets and camp chairs already lined the curb. A street sweeper came toward her, and she could hear the white noise of its continuous sweep, picking up old chip bags, hardened gum, cigarette butts. It was Labor Day, and by noon the street would be filled with people celebrating the day off with elephant ears and flower crowns, watching the parade pass by. She wondered where she should go for the best view. Several of the older businesses had stoops, but the ice cream parlor's steps had thick cement sloping sides that functioned as handrails and looked like the perfect perch for seeing everything from behind and yet over the crowd of strangers. She decided to get there a bit early and bring a small throw quilt from the room to save her spot.

Now that she had a plan for her last day here, she headed back up the hill to her turret room and a hot shower.

*   *   *

Her face in the mirror surprised her as the mist dissipated enough to show her reflection; it was red from the sun and the hot water, but the bump on her forehead had shrunk significantly - so much that it could probably be easily covered with a strategic sweep of her bangs. She dressed in her holiday red, white, and blue, grabbed her American flag on a stick, put Goliath on his leash, and headed downstairs.

Moira was ready for her in a floral housecoat with snaps from the neck to the hem. Snaps. Only babies and older people used snaps. They were such a satisfying fastener; she wondered why people in the middle years avoided them. Just then Moira leaned over the table to place a platter of croissants in the middle of the table on the lace doily, and her ample bosom popped the third snap down. That's why. They could not be relied upon.

"Oopsie! Unintentional flashing. Sorry," Moira giggled. "Once when I was swimming in Lake Michigan as a teenager, I stood up and waved to my friends on the beach. They waved and pointed back at me, laughing. I looked down and noticed that the lake had run off with my bikini top! It was so funny that I almost wasn't embarrassed. My best friend brought me out a towel, and we laughed and laughed. Modesty isn't really my thing. You know, the sixties."

"You're in your sixties now? Or the 1960s?" Beth smiled.

"Both!"

"I sometimes wish I could have lived back then. The 'eighties were far less cool, and less free to grow up in. Families were more stable back then, too, weren't they?"

"Oh, I don't know. I think they hid their secrets better. As time goes on, I think we went from hiding, to revealing, to flaunting. Now everyone's got to share prit'near every dinner they eat with all their online *friends* – tell me, Beth, is that really necessary? Does anyone really care what I eat for lunch?"

"Probably not, but I care a lot about this breakfast you made. Can you pass me the hard-boiled eggs?"

"Sure thing, dear. Are you goin' to the parade?"

"Yes. I have my spot all picked out." She cracked the egg and sliced it onto her buttered wheat toast. "Are you?"

"Nah, too crowded. I'm liable to run into a bunch of people who want to catch up, and then I won't have any time to make dinner. Will you be eating here tonight? I'll take a picture of your food and post it on the wall somewhere if that will make it more fun." She smirked. "I have an old Polaroid camera for instant pictures. You just have to shake it a little." She did a little hip-waggle. Beth laughed and then got serious.

"Yes, I plan to. Then, right after, unfortunately, I'll have to pack up and head out. I've got an hour drive back to the city and work in the morning. It was a lovely getaway though. Can I come back soon?"

"I'd be sad if you didn't. I'll bet you are just the age my daughter would have been. It's been so nice having you here. Most people who come are couples that don't have any time or need to chit-chat with me."

"Well, I'll come for sure then." Beth rolled that phrase over in her mind *would have been*. Secrets indeed. She sensed that chipping away at that story would be easy with someone soft like Moira. Another time though. Friendships moved slowly for Beth. It was hard to move the bins that built her walls. It was safer inside. She had never taken a picture of her dinner to share on social media. She didn't even have an account. She tried once, but it asked her what she wanted to share. And she didn't want to share. She could carry her baggage alone.

*　　*　　*

The crowd had started to gather. They were plopped down on blankets and chairs next to coolers of drinks and snacks, waiting for the show. Beth claimed her spot and then turned and went inside to get an ice cream. It was one of those pre-fall days that feels like October with a chill in the air and a breeze blowing down the main street like it was a wind tunnel. Before long she would be using the quilt she brought as a wrap instead of a cushion. But it was the perfect day for ice cream. The cool air would keep it from melting, so it could be enjoyed slowly, without the constant drip-licking required on a scorching day.

Inside the ice cream parlor, it smelled like sugar and vanilla and waffles, like childhood. The marble counter may have been an actual old-time soda fountain, and the ceiling was squares of punched tin. It would have been nostalgic if the sounds had been the echo of the click of high heels instead of the dull thwap of the ubiquitous flip flop. The sound of it assaulted her ears. *People wear them to work now.* She found it absurd, *slovenly.*

"Could I get two scoops of butter pecan in a waffle cone?" Beth asked the willowy teenager behind the counter.

"Of course," the teenager said, barely looking up.

While she watched the girl scoop her ice cream, she wondered where the awkwardness had gone. When she was in high school most kids had serious acne, bad fashion, worse perms, and oh, my, the bangs! These millennials seemed to skip that stage entirely, dressed in timeless pieces to complement their clear skin and perfectly straightened bang-less hair. They would probably laugh out loud at the damage done to her already unmanageable teenage hair by a crimping iron. Whose bad idea was that contraption?

"That'll be four fifty."

"Right, here you go. Happy Labor Day."

"Yep." and she moved on to the next person in line, while she wiped her sticky fingers with a washcloth and rolled her perfectly lined eyes. Some things were the same.

From her stoop-perch, Beth could pull her knees up and almost disappear. She watched the clouds for a while, then the people caught her attention. A parade crowd is full of endless diversity and interest. To her right there was a family with two little kids, maybe one and three. They were sitting in a wagon with a pile of snacks and toys between them. The three-year-old picked up the pinwheel and started to blow softly. It turned a quarter turn and stopped. She had turned her head to look at a clown, strolling down the empty street, making balloon animals for the kids. Her eyes got wide, but she decided that clowns were not worth the risk and turned back to her pinwheel only to find her little brother blowing at it frantically, bits of granola bar flying onto the metallic petals and sticking. She wrinkled her nose and proceeded to bop him on the head with it. His chubby fingers grabbed at it and closed around the flower end, crushing the delicate curves and rendering it useless. Her tears could not make it pretty again, any more than one could return an overstretched slinky to its original shape for stair-hopping. So, she relinquished her toy to him and crossed her arms over her belly and sighed heavily, sliding down in her seat and resting her head on the side of the wagon to show how very done she was with this parade that hadn't yet begun.

Their parents, no doubt exhausted by the struggle of getting two small children and their accoutrements to a parade, on time, seemed truly oblivious to the entire altercation, holding hands and smiling into the late-summer sun.

In striking contrast, to Beth's left was an elderly couple. They had glistening silver hair and sat comfortably in a stiff tandem camp chair with a small table built in between them. On the table was a small bag full of lavender yarn and two large, long knitting needles. Once they were settled, the lady took them out and proceeded to serenely knit, then purl, making what looked like a scarf, or one strip of a blanket. The man sat peacefully, a cup of coffee in a Styrofoam cup with a lid, sipping gingerly so as not to burn his tongue. They needed no pinwheels, drama, or even conversation. Beth imagined they had been together so long that everything had already been said and was understood between them.

Just then the first organized marchers were seen coming around the corner and toward them. The parade began with trumpets, then soldiers, one with an American flag and long tassels on a brass pole. The end of the pole was fitted into a special pocket on the soldier's belt. Behind him was the high school marching band in red, white, and blue uniforms playing

"The Star-Spangled Banner." Most sat and clapped, having just gotten comfortable on their blankets and chairs, but the old man put down his coffee, giving the arms of his chair a death grip, and, standing straight with obvious effort, saluted as they passed by. Inspired by his gravitas, Beth slipped off her railing to the top step and stood as well, quietly mouthing the words of the anthem, just as Goliath poked his head out of her blue, star-spangled handbag. As the band passed by and she sat, she scooped Goliath up onto her lap, scratching him behind his ears and humming the anthem softly.

She felt her newfound peace was to be only short-lived as her impending return home this afternoon would be a return to all she had been trying to escape from. In her growing anxiety, her eyes darted from stranger to stranger, not taking time to examine them. They were simply colors and shapes, a sea of patriotism and small-town pride.

Then, from the sea, emerged an odd buoy of familiarity and anomaly, a face strangely recognizable and yet mildly contorted. She gasped. *Adam.* He struggled to maneuver through the crowds. His clothes were rumpled and may have been the same he was wearing when she met him yesterday. He kept running his hand through his already tousled and unruly hair to push it back from his face because he had to keep looking down to avoid stepping on fingers, strangers' blankets, dog tails. The effort it took him to make his way through the crowd must have become too much, because he turned toward the road, just across the street from her and began walking through a family, awkwardly apologizing and stumbling.

He then stood on the car-less street in the gap between spectators and parade, swaying a bit and looking unsure of where to go from there.   The next float in the parade temporarily blocked him from her view. Once it passed, Beth saw him striding purposefully toward a man in a three-piece suit, walking behind a red banner that read, "State Senator, George Murray." He was crossing from one side of the road to another, shaking hands, kissing babies, and handing out pencils to the children that said "Re-elect Murray, Families First." He was so intent on his campaigning, that he didn't notice the man coming up behind him, red-faced and unsteady. Beth's hand went to cover her mouth.

As the senator turned to refill his handful of pencils from the bucket his assistant carried, his eyes got large, and he ducked just in time to avoid the fist, flying at his right ear, landing squarely in the shoulder of the assistant. Pencils flew through the air and rolled to the side of the street. Children jumped up to grab them as parents tried to hold them back so they wouldn't be collateral damage in this bizarre spectacle. One tow-headed boy held twenty pencils in his little hand like a bouquet, smiling like a Cheshire cat while his mother bit her lip in confusion and struggled to get him back onto their blanket.

On the street, the senator reacted by bouncing back with an uppercut to Adam's chin. His head flew back as if his spine was made of rubber, and he was lying on the cement, bleeding, staring at the sky.

Beth immediately jumped up and was down the stairs and in the street in a moment. Not accustomed to calling attention to herself, she wondered *why on earth am I doing this*, and yet, she was. She kneeled beside him and moved her index finger back and forth in front of his eyes as she'd seen done on emergency room shows, and his eyes followed her finger. She called to some men on the curb to please help, and they lifted Adam off the pavement together and carried him over to the small grassy area beside the gas station and laid him down. When she looked up, the senator was a block down the street, smiling and waving as though nothing had happened, a trace of blood on the knuckles of his right hand.

"I have to go get Goliath," she said, holding up one finger to indicate that she'd only be a minute.

"Okay. I'll be here," he said, his head falling back into the dry grass.

She practically ran back to the ice cream shop, grabbed her quilt and her handbag, and returned to his side. She tried not to notice the looks she was getting as she did but couldn't ignore the fact that if invisible was the look she was going for, she had failed. Over the next week, there would not be a soul in town that hadn't heard of her. She would be discussed in conversations over coffee, back fences, ballet lessons. They would wonder where she came from and who she was. They would discuss in hushed tones how she knew Adam, the middle school counselor, and whether or not she knew Dominique, his wife. They would remark on her toned calves and her patriotic ensemble; they would decide things about which they knew nothing.

They would tear her apart.

*   *   *

"What was that?" Beth asked.

"What?" Adam replied.

"Are you against pencils on principle?"

"Ha!" he laughed and then rubbed his bleeding chin. "I hate that guy. He's robbing schools of their funding, giving it to his cronies in business. I am the only school counselor in the whole middle school. Nine hundred students, all with their own issues. Just me to try to help them. There aren't enough hours in the day."

"So you thought you'd punch him?"

"I needed to punch someone. His smug face...I just couldn't help it. This is *Labor Day*. He has no idea what labor is. He doesn't know what it's done for him, for everyone. He looks like upper management. This day isn't for him. It's for them." He propped himself up on his elbow and pointed to the crowd. They were still watching the parade, but now they had their side-eye on him as well.

"How are *you*? Is your head okay? You really caught me on a bad weekend. I normally don't go around concussing everyone I see."

"I'll be fine. Can you walk, do you think? Do you wanna go get some coffee? I don't mean to be rude, but you reek of a distillery and could probably use some." She dipped down and hooked her shoulder under his armpit to help him up. He groaned a bit but rose slowly. There was dead grass stuck in the back of his hair, but he didn't brush it away. He put his hands on his knees, bending forward.

Oh no, she thought, *he's going to be sick.*

But he just breathed deeply and stood up straight. They walked together down the crowded sidewalk, past snack vendors and racks of clothes from the local boutiques, to the end of the block and a cozy little coffee shop called Beantown. Walking inside, the aroma of freshly ground beans and pastries filled the room. The wood floors creaked a little. The walls were covered with large, framed photographs of Fenway Park, Old North Church, the USS Constitution. There was a pleasant mixture of furniture, like a giant great room. The dented copper counter sparkled, and the barista they ordered from had a thick Bostonian accent.

"Would you like some dahrk chahklit syrup with that? It's our specialty."

"No thanks. Just soy milk," Beth replied.

"This place is great," she said to Adam as they sat across from each other in a corner booth, "beats Starbucks by a mile."

"Yeah, they really went with the theme. I admire that kind of commitment."

"It's clever."

"She's re-creating home. It's primal. And who moves from Boston to suburban Detroit? It's great here and all, but she must miss Boston is all I'm saying."

"Probably." There was a long, awkward silence as they sipped their drinks and looked at each other, unsure how to proceed from their brief acquaintance with its weirdly violent beginning.

"Are we gonna talk about the drunk elephant in the room?" Beth asked.

"Do you want to?" he replied, leaning sideways, his ear resting in his palm.

"Maybe. To be honest, when I meet new people, I don't usually dig too deeply. But you seem to be carrying a lot of baggage, maybe that you're trying to unload? I have suitcases of my own, and I'm not sure that I need a friend that badly," Beth replied honestly, but the fact that she was opening up even this much gave her pause. "You said you're a school counselor?"

"Yes."

"I am talking a lot more than you. Am I on a metaphorical couch?"

"Sorry, occupational hazard. Do you want me to unload *my* suitcases? Make this a conversation, not a session?"

"Maybe a little? You just seem like a really nice guy, even with all the evidence to the contrary. I guess maybe a little explanation would help ease my mind."

"Okay. My wife, well -- "

She had been right to assume a wife, of course she had been. Why else would he be throwing a closet full of beautiful things onto the lawn? Then she looked at his left hand closely for the first time and saw a pale circle where his ring had been. It had obviously been worn most of the summer.

He took a deep breath. "I'm not enough for her. I mean, I don't make enough for her. She wants expensive things. Things I can't afford. She found someone who can." He slumped so his cheek was touching his bicep. He spoke in a raspy whisper. "I confronted her last night. Then I spent the rest of it on the business end of a beer bottle. I haven't been to sleep since before we met yesterday, but I haven't been sleeping for a while. I'm at the end of my ability to give a shit. I don't know what to do."

Beth thought for a minute. She thought about her penchant for the baggage of others. She thought about his needs and her own. This friendship could be mutually beneficial. And those eyes. She could stare into them all day, like a storm, closing in.

"What do you need? Right now," Beth asked.

He took this question seriously, rolled it over in his head. "Fun."

"The midway it is," she said, and they paid the check and headed out the door, down the side street toward the Ferris wheel they could see reaching up out of the city park.

*   *   *

Dominique walked the side streets, avoiding the crowds. She was weary. On the one hand, it was a relief for the truth to be out in the open, but on the other, new anxieties floated up from the depths of her consciousness. *Would he leave her? Could this be fixed? Did she want it to be? What was it that she really wanted? What would the future hold?* As she ruminated on the hot mess of her life, she had stopped paying attention to her feet, and her sandal caught on the uneven sidewalk, sending her forward with an awkward movement that looked as though she was trying to catch a frisbee. She didn't fall but looked around quickly to see if anyone had seen her trip. There was no one. Relieved, she kept walking with increased attention.

She passed a garage sale. Generally, garage sales are pretty pathetic on the third day, but Dominique really wasn't a garage-saler anyway. She really couldn't understand why anyone would pay actual money for someone else's cast-offs. Did they value themselves so cheaply? Had they given up? Today was full of unanswered questions, and it was easier to judge than self-reflect. She passed a house with an old playpen, a plastic bathtub, and a stained bouncy seat in the driveway. Next to them was a card table with a few folded snapsuits and jammies for infants. There was also a small, quilted blanket, a little dirty on the corners. She picked it up, brought it to her face and inhaled. It smelled like baby. Talcum powder, spoiled milk, and Johnson's shampoo.

She had had a blanket like this. As a child. It was a comfort on many dark nights. The one thing that had always been with her. Her mother had left it with her. When she left her.

She put the blanket down and walked back home. The empty house was not a refuge. Its Spartan décor did not feel homey or soft or warm. It looked like a museum of modern furniture, as though no one lived here but the *desire to look cool* and its brother *soulless stylish.* Adam still hadn't returned. She went up to the attic, found her box of childhood things. She dug through the old school papers and trophies, and there it was, quilted from a hundred different scraps of fabric, torn and worn and soft and perfect. She looked at the carefully hand-sewn seams and wondered about the woman who had labored over them. *Was it a gift? Did her mother make it for her, resting it on her round belly as she planned for a future with her daughter that would never be?* She brought it to her bed, spread it over her pillow, inhaling what she imagined to be her own faint baby scent, soaking up the afternoon sun like a cat on a windowsill, and fell asleep.

*   *   *

On the other side of town, Beth and Adam walked through the empty lot the girls' basketball team was using as a parking lot fundraiser, only $5 per car. The grass was crushed and brown and the lot was dusty from the preceding string of hot days. From the park wafted the strong aroma of baked pretzels, deep-fried dough, and porta-potties.

"Well, what kind of carnival girl are you?"

"I can't go on any spin-y rides, unless you'd like to see the ice cream I ate earlier, but I love carnival food, within reason. What is up with deep-fried Oreos?" He gave her a mystified look as if the concept of putting that concoction into his mouth was an impossibility. "And I love carnival games. I secretly long for a giant pink sparkly unicorn. I sometimes play when they have parking lot carnivals at the Kmart down the road from my house but have never won anything bigger than a disappointing consolation prize. I'm pretty sure they're rigged."

"You think?" He smirked. "Well, I think, since you saved me this afternoon, I'd like to repay you in sparkly unicorn. I can't promise, but I did play baseball in high school, maybe I could knock down the pyramid of cans."

"Or maybe not," he said fifteen minutes and fifty dollars later. He hung his head in defeat.

"I'm pretty sure they're rigged," she said again, and elbowed him gently.

"Settle for lemonade and the Ferris wheel?"

"Okay." They waited in line at the ticket window, then the food truck window, then the Ferris wheel. Both of them were watching the crowd, shaking their heads at the Daisy Dukes and filthy feet in dollar store flip flops. The line at the Ferris wheel is always the longest since they can't let everyone off at once. And then, just as the silence was starting to get awkward, Beth asked, "What kind of carnival boy are you?"

"I just like to wander around and watch, to study the people and the relationships walking by. I like to imagine the lives of the carnival workers, moving all the time, out in the hot sun. What do their kids do? Do they go to school?"

"I never thought of that. Maybe they have tutors? It's hard to do that kind of watching from the Ferris wheel, sure you want to go?"

"Oh, yeah. I need to shift my focus from all these strangers to my knight in shining red, white and blue."

"Want some wine with that cheese? Relax. I can't run off for at least 10 minutes without seriously injuring myself," Beth said. The carnival worker clicked the metal barrier shut and knocked on it to let the operator know it was secure. There was a bit of a backward lurch, and they were gliding forward and up, then backward and down. The best thing about a Ferris wheel is the view.

"I can see my room from here!" Beth said, pointing to the turret up the hill.

"It sure is beautiful and peaceful up here."

"The last time I was on a Ferris wheel was at Navy Pier in Chicago. The wind was so strong, I had to hold on to the sides to keep from blowing out. I swear, it was so scary. This is nicer. There isn't any wind, and I'm not alone."

"You rode at Navy Pier alone? Why?"

"That's how I do most things." Goliath poked his head out of her handbag, as if offended. "Well, just me and Goliath. I keep to myself."

"Why didn't you leave me lying in the road then?"

"I don't know. I guess it was because you picked me up and brought me inside when *I* fell."

"Yeah, but that was my fault. Actually, they both were."

"Yes, but I felt a connection, in your living room. That's not a regular thing for me. I was hoping we could be friends."

"We are," he said simply. "I owe you. More than one."

The ride swooped to a stop, and they got out, a little wobbly.

"I hate to do this, but I really have to hit the road. I've already stayed longer than I intended," Beth said.

"Okay. Let me just try one more game, quickly, please? I need to redeem myself."

"I really only have time for one."

Adam pulled a quarter out of his pocket and headed over to the quarter pitch. There were eleven clear glass plates on sticks, a red one right in the middle. He just had to get his quarter to land on one and not bounce off. He turned to Beth, closed his eyes, made a wish, and flipped the coin up and over his head to the plates behind him. It hit the foot of a giant stuffed zebra, fell down onto a plate, bounced up and slightly back, and landed in the center of the red middle plate and skidded to a stop. He jumped, yelled, smiled. The red plate was a choice of all the biggest animals.

"I would like the pink sparkly unicorn please!" Beth said.

"Here you go, miss," the carnival man replied, unhooking it from a giant S hook hanging from a chain. Beth hugged it tightly.

"Thank you," she said to *Steve*, the carnival man, and to Adam, "We're even."

Adam winked, and they walked back to town. The parade was over now, and people were milling about, dodging traffic. As they said goodbye, Beth asked, "Can I call you? You know, if I'm in town again?"

"I hope you do. I promise to be better behaved."

She turned to go, started walking, then stopped and turned around for a last look. He hadn't moved. He was watching her walk away, standing there in the sidewalk as if he had nowhere to go.

*   *   *

Back at Moira's B&B, Beth sat on the bedspread and folded the quilt and put it back on the shelf in the closet. She packed her things quickly and went downstairs to say goodbye. She peeked into the sunroom. Moira's back was to her, she was working on something, but Beth couldn't see what it was.

"Moira?" Beth whispered so as not to startle her. Moira turned, a lace tablecloth in her lap, ripped a little on the seam.

"Oh, hello, dear. I'm just mending this lace. It's so delicate that it seems any little catch causes a lace-tastrophe! One of the other guest's belt buckle got caught. Not important now though." She put the tablecloth down, got up, and gave Beth a bear hug. "Can I send you home with any good love stories?"

"No, thank you. I don't really think it's my genre."

"Suit yourself. Please drive carefully and come back soon. Do you need any Advil for that head bonk? It looks so much better today, but sometimes those things leave behind a headache."

"I think I'm fine, but thanks. I'm actually feeling really good today. Maybe better than I have in a while. Maybe I needed a head bonk."

"Sometimes a shoe to the head will knock some sense into you," Moira said and smiled, "not that I'm saying you're low on sense."

"If only you knew," Beth said, and winked. She had never winked at anyone before. She was pretty sure her wink's execution was awkward, but she was feeling playful. "I'll definitely be back."

"I'll leave the light on for you. Figuratively, of course, no one needs to waste that much electricity."

Beth grabbed her bag, Goliath's leash, and her giant unicorn and headed for the door. Moira opened it for her, shaking her head at the silly silhouette of the retreating figures, hoping for the best for them. Beth strapped the unicorn into the back seat, threw her bag in the way back, and let Goliath hop up into shotgun. She waved as she drove away, pretty proud that she had only acquired five more things while she was here. A scarf, a book, a bucket, a unicorn, and a friend. But being who she was, she wouldn't let any of them go.

*   *   *

The drive home was peaceful. She watched the sunset through the apple trees; Goliath snored a little, curled up on the passenger seat with the seat warmer on high, and when Beth checked her blind spot, she was rewarded with a sparkly pink smile. It was going to be a challenge going back to her solitary *real life,* but she was definitely rejuvenated by a chance to escape from her fortress, interact with people, and focus on someone else's problems for a while.

As she walked into her house, it seemed darker than before. There was no turret, only a dungeon. She had to push her unicorn through the narrow walkway. When she finally got to her sunken family room and curled up on her pull-out couch that couldn't be pulled out, she left the unicorn on the floor next to her. Goliath jumped up on it and moved around until he got comfortable. She was so tired. So...tired...

Chapter 7

To seek connection in a divided world is hope.

Beth's run the next morning was uncomfortable. First, she was attempting to run with a metal bucket. Second, all she could think of was how she was going to give a gift to a girl whose name she didn't know. Third, what kind of weirdo would the girl's parents think she was? She did something she never did at the entrance to the cul-du-sac; she stopped. Feeling stupid, she stood there all sweaty with the bucket in her hands. *What was she doing?* She turned to go back home, then remembered jumping up from the stoop to scoop Adam from the concrete. She was courageous and idiotic *yesterday*. She could be courageous and idiotic today. She turned back around and looked down the street to the house. The grass was still tall, but the area between the street and the road had been cut, maybe by the city. It was like an invitation.

The first time she stopped on this street to check her pulse, she stood right in front of the house. The windows were wide open, even though it was drizzling, and the condition of the house and yard had caught her attention. She desperately wanted to trim and mow and scrape and paint. That's when she heard it. It started softly, just the strumming of an acoustic guitar. Then came a softer man's voice soon joined by a woman's and a child's. They sang about their new little family, their empty pockets, the love that would sustain and connect them.

Loggins and Messina sang it beautifully, but these voices put them to shame. Those people wouldn't judge her.

She jogged up to the front door. She knocked before thinking any more about it, and the screen door shook without a latch to hold it steady. A woman's face appeared at the door, and while she appeared confused by the visitor, she swung the door open wide.

"Can I help you?"

"Um, this is going to sound really odd, but I run through this neighborhood every day, and last week, I met your daughter on the sidewalk. She told me about her bucket list and her overflowing bucket. While I was away this weekend, I found a perfect one at an antique store and bought it for her on impulse. Is that too weird? I can go." Beth made an apologetic face and turned to the door.

"Wait, don't you want to give it to her yourself?" The woman turned and yelled upstairs, "Danny! You have a visitor!" Then to Beth, "Can I get you a glass of water? Your face is red. How far do you run?"

"I live just five miles west of here, on Charlevoix Drive."

"What?! You run ten miles? In a row? Are you Wonder Woman?" she asked, walking backward into the kitchen. Her mouth was still wide with awe as she poured a glass and set it on the table.

"It clears my head."

"I think you're clean out of your head, but that's because I'm lazy at my core. The sloth is my kindred spirit. Oh, and I'm rude," she said, wiping her hands on her jeans and offering her right to Beth, "my name is Kendra."

"Beth. Happy to meet you."

Just then a familiar face peeked surreptitiously around the corner into the tidy 1950s kitchen. Her eyes got even bigger when she spotted Beth. "Hi! Come to play polo?"

"No, although that sounds lovely. I actually remembered this weekend that you were needing a new bucket for your list, and I found this one. Would you like it?"

Danny nodded vigorously and inspected the metal bucket with the seriousness of a scientist in a lab.

"Is your name Danny, did I hear your mom say?"

"Short for Daniela. But Danny suits me better, or that's what everyone says."

"Well, I don't mean to disrupt your morning, and I need to get to work, but it was awfully nice finally officially meeting you. Both of you."

"Thank you, Ms. Beth," Danny said, and threw her arms around Beth's middle. "The bucket is just what I needed. I finally found the blue one in the yard, but it was broken. I think maybe a polo player hit it with her mallet? But you didn't hear that from me."

Beth and Kendra exchanged smiles over Danny's head.

"Stop by anytime," Kendra added. "We have lots of water. Just don't ask me to join you unless we're walking to DQ."

"Thank you, really."

As the screen door crashed shut behind her, Beth looked at the cracked steps with even more love. These people hadn't judged her bizarre behavior. They hadn't scowled at her for being at their door or looked worried that she was stalking their daughter. They took in kindness like they gave it out. They trusted people to be good. Trusted them with their open conversation, unlocked doors, wide smiles.

Back on the road, that burden lifted and bucket-less, Beth sailed across the concrete sidewalk squares. She didn't know who she was back there, or how she did it, but things seemed to be looking up. She wondered where Danny's father was. She would have liked to see the face that went with that voice, but baby steps would have to do. Honestly, this weekend they felt like Baby Huey steps. *I may have to dig in my garage for a bucket of my own.* Dreaming of a future unlike her past was a luxury Beth seldom allowed herself, but today it felt possible. Today she was Wonder Woman.

Then it occurred to her. She had given something away. She had owned something and without a second thought had handed it over to someone else, someone who needed it, someone who got joy from the receiving. It would not be added to the pile. It would not later have to be moved so that she could walk up her stairs or through a hallway. It would live out its life elsewhere, in a place that seemed less inviting from the outside but in fact was the inverse of her world. She imagined it perched on a desk next to a diary with a small locking clasp and a jewelry box that, when opened, showcased a jingly song and a twirling ballerina. Danny would be there on the fluffy floor rug shaped like Holly Hobbie, pillow behind her head as she stared up at the constellations on her ceiling, hundreds of glow-in-the-dark stickers meant to mimic the night sky. Maybe there were shelves of books full of old favorites, *Where the Wild Things Are, The Bobbsey Twins, The Pink and Blue Fairy Books,* maybe even *The Boxcar Children.* The pages might be dog-eared and the covers faded; there may be little drawings in

84

the margins. But it was the stuff inside that was valuable; that's where the heart is. She would have to rethink the cover of her own book and just who was judging her by it.

* * *

As she walked in the door, Goliath jumped down from the unicorn belly and skidded to a stop on the tile at her feet. She refilled his water and food bowls and let him outside to run a bit while she showered. Let loose on the front lawn, Goliath immediately went into sentry mode, pacing back and forth looking for litter. They had been gone for several days, and it was obvious. Beth's usually obsessive trimming, weeding, and mowing had been neglected long enough that her yard looked like everyone else's. Like she had better things to do.

Still, trash could not be tolerated. Goliath raced to a glint in the corner of the yard. It was a tiny bottle, just right for him to pick up and carry. He immediately did as he had been taught and headed for the dog door and the front porch.

Tony lived around the corner from Beth and had just lost his job. He wasn't a drinker; his parents, his wife, his daughter wouldn't approve. He didn't approve. But today he was trying to soothe the fear inside him. He needed to know how he would send his little girl to college, pay the mortgage, eat. He was living paycheck to paycheck like most of the neighborhood, so he spent a bit of his last one on a hotel pack of mini-bar peppermint schnapps. The scent might be mistaken for breath mints, or mouthwash, he reasoned. He drank it as close to home as he could, so he would be in the garage and not drunk driving by the time it hit his stomach, throwing the evidence into Beth's yard. The next day, when he saw it was already gone, he made an imaginary pact with Goliath – clean up the evidence, and I'll make sure you have something to do. After a few weeks, Beth's Front Lawn Litter box looked more like a hotel room recycle bin after a bender. But Tony kept "driving to work" every morning, unable to break the news to his family -- littering every afternoon, unable to admit that his fear had become an even bigger problem. It wouldn't be long now, and the checks would start to bounce. The power would get shut off; the life they had built would crumble. Everyone knows there is no tired like newborn baby parent tired, but even though his daughter was seven, sleepless nights and wandering the streets all day looking for work were taking their toll, wearing him down as the box on Beth's front porch filled up, a mountain of peppermint sadness. A pyramid that may outlast those in Giza.

Chapter 8

"The truth is rarely pure and never simple." – Oscar Wilde *The Importance of Being Earnest*

When Dominique woke up the next morning, Adam was sitting on the beige chaise by the window. His eyes were bloodshot. His chin was swollen and covered with stubble. There was blood on his shirt.

"You look like you've been through hell."

"This is nothing. You should see my heart."

"I've seen it. It's lovely."

"You wrecked it."

"I'm sorry."

"Are you done with him?"

"I don't know."

"Then you're not sorry."

"But I love you," she protested.

"Not enough," he whispered.

"I don't love you enough?"

"No, your love is not enough. It's cheap, Dom. If it can be bought for a handbag."

They just sat there, breathing in their regret and disappointment.

"I gave *you* my love for free," she said.

"It's costing me."

She stood up. "I'll go. For a while. If you want."

"Take it with you."

"What?"

"Your fancy stuff. Your collateral. I can't have it here."

"Okay."

She slipped into the closet, dressed, packed her bag. Downstairs, she threw in the pile still stacked on the dining room table and slipped out the door into the morning.

Adam lay back on the chaise and looked around the room. The bed and chaise were the only furniture. To most people it would look like they hadn't really moved in, like they were visitors in their own lives, but Adam preferred it this way. He liked a bare room. He didn't need stuff, fancy or otherwise. He needed sleep. He called in sick to school and crawled into bed. As he brought his arm up under his head, he noticed Dom's baby blanket. It was so colorful in the stark room, it felt wrong, but he loved the roughness of all the seams; he loved the earthy smell. He loved the idea of his baby wife and the chubby arms that were wrapped in it. This one thing could stay.

*   *   *

The next day, when Adam walked into Chesapeake Middle School, he went straight to his office to try to get his mind off the weekend and focus on helping his students. Usually sociable, he avoided making eye contact with anyone. It wasn't difficult as most of his colleagues were in the copy room, discussing the scene at the parade, looking furtively around to make sure Adam, and especially students, couldn't hear them.

Jan, the secretary, said, "Did anyone see it in person?"

"I did. It was unsettling," said Amy, the sixth-grade history teacher.

"What happened, exactly?"

"He looked terrible. He stumbled out onto the street and tried to assault Representative Murray. He missed but hit another guy. Pencils went flying."

"Pencils?"

"Yeah, some propaganda tool. My kids tried to run out and get them, but I held them back."

"That Murray is a tool." Jim, the eighth-grade math teacher said, "I can't believe he keeps getting re-elected for promising to keep family first, but then steals money from kids to fund his cronies. I've had visions of punching him myself, but I can't believe Adam actually took a swing."

"Well, the thing that I found so bananas is that then Murray turned around and punched him so hard he was knocked out cold. Then this random woman in the crowd came out and helped him off. I didn't see Dominique anywhere. I've never seen the lady before. She was really pretty, though--" Amy said.

Just then the principal walked in, and they dispersed to their classrooms, still buzzing.

*   *   *

Adam sat in his office, clean-shaven but shaken. His head was in his hands, and he was looking at the list of kids that he needed to see. The first one had a melt-down last week because she got a B+ on her math quiz. He had spoken with her then, but she hadn't been very receptive. She had been unable to control her sobs and her puffy red face was wet with tears. She refused to understand after he repeatedly explained that a B+ was above average, that her grades didn't determine her value, and that everything would be fine. He wanted to follow up with her and make sure that she had moved past it.

When she poked her head in, Mr. Connors straightened up in his chair. "Hi, Molly, how are you this beautiful Wednesday morning? Did you talk to your parents about last week? What did they say?"

She dutifully answered his questions, it seemed that mom and dad had talked her off the proverbial ledge. "Mr. Connors?"

"Yes?"

"Are you okay?"

"What do you mean?"

"Well, I heard some things in the hall yesterday when you weren't here. People are saying lots of stuff. The kids here, though, we've got your back. Just so you know. We know you're a good guy, okay?"

"Thanks, Molly. That really means a lot to me." He was starting to tear up. "Go ahead and get back to class, don't want you to miss anything."

"Okay." She turned and looked straight into his soggy eyes, "It's going to be fine. You'll see." She left his office with that half-skipping, half-running gait that adolescents can't seem to contain, all legs and arms and possibility.

*   *   *

Beth spent the week in the same, monotonous routine she had used for decades. She ran, she worked, she gardened. She tried to sleep more but didn't sleep enough. She avoided her house by taking Goliath for walks and shopping. She got coffee and drank it alone. Leaning on the arm of the Starbucks couch, she planned her next trip to Chesapeake without making any reservations or actual commitments. It wasn't Beantown, but she loved the people who maintained their aloofness, leaving her alone to ponder and sip without trying to make friends or involve her in their lives in any way. Even the baristas here barely talked except to ask for her order and her name. Small town hospitality was wonderful, unless, like Beth, one really wanted to be ignored. Once the weekend arrived, however, it was more difficult to fill those empty hours. Her lawn was taken care of, for now; the serious raking would begin soon, and it was raining. Not a warm summer rain that barely dampens the spirits, but rather a cold, horizontal rain that would, if she were to go out in it, cause her to spend the entire afternoon trying to get warm again. So, although she was loathe to be trapped in her house all day, she resigned herself to it.

"Goliath, do you want to try to clean out the bedroom? Make space so we can stop sleeping down here in the living room? I swear my back is suffering from the couch sleeping, and I never feel really rested, even right after I wake up. That turret room spoiled me." These conversations were always one-sided, of course, but Beth didn't seem to mind. Goliath always looked right at her when she spoke to him, which is much more than she could say for most humans. They always seemed annoyed if she said something important enough that they felt obligated to look up from their stupid smart phones. This one-sided conversation had a downside, though, when she did interact with people. She was nearly always caught off guard when someone responded to a question or a comment she made, and it left the impression that she was skittish, and slightly inattentive, which wasn't true at all.

She side-stepped up the stairs. The right side of every step had two or three large Rubbermaid tubs on it. The left side had a railing that just served to push Beth closer to the piles and what could really be a dangerous situation if she fell because there was nothing to stop her from riding on plastic lids all the way to the wall at the bottom. Because of this, Beth always side-stepped with her back to the wall with the railing and held on tightly. Goliath scurried up behind her, probably wondering what on earth they were going to do up here.

At her door, she paused. It had been months since she had dared venture upstairs, much less into this room that was supposed to be her sanctuary. She turned the knob and pushed. It didn't swing wide like Danny and Kendra's screen door, in fact, there was so much resistance, Beth could only open it less than ten inches. She squeezed through the opening. She thought, what if I get trapped in here? No one will ever find me. She shooed Goliath out into the hall, afraid he would get lost, and she shut the door.

What she saw made her shake her head. It would take days, maybe weeks to make this room livable again. There were crates and boxes against each wall, but they weren't filled with clothes, as one might expect in a bedroom, because Beth had moved all her clothes downstairs years ago to prevent endangering herself on the stairs. Instead, there were books, and figurines, boxes of toys from her childhood, both houses, so there were lots of duplicates. She had two tea sets, two teddy bears, two jewelry boxes. A Noah's Ark of misery. This, and the sugar cubes, may have been the beginning. When her parents died, because she was an only child, she got everything. Her own childhood things, but theirs too. It all meant something to her. She was so in awe of them, so frightened by their powerful personalities, that she didn't have the courage to throw out their things.

Beth crawled up a sliding pile where the shoe bench had been and struggled to sit on the Mount Everest her bed had become. She didn't want to plant a flag claiming it for herself; she wanted to pretend it wasn't even part of her realm or maybe knock it down so she could start over with the clean slate of a barren field. An empty space that she didn't need to fill. She was ready to make a change, so she sat down, right in the middle, and started to dig. Leaning up against the headboard was a tall stack of papers. She flipped through the pages. It was from college, her undergrad at Belladonna University. On top was an essay she had written analyzing Juliet's immaturity to show Shakespeare's immaturity. She read through it and saw her own immaturity, weak comparisons, foregone and easy conclusions. Underneath the English papers were stacks of blue books full of essay tests that she had labored over four hours at a time. She had sat there trying to recall, tie together, and apply a whole semester's worth of ideas – to make them mean more together than each one did alone.

This pile, these papers, these memories didn't do that though. They didn't tie together and make her life a solution; they just stacked up to hide the problem. Alone her ideas may have been good. They may have moved her forward, but together, here in a pile where she should be able to sleep, they were a landfill avalanche, pushing her backward faster than she could dig herself out.

"Enough of this!" she yelled into the air. She picked up the closest blue book and ripped it in half. "I wrote these ideas down twenty years ago! Why can't I let them go?" She started to cry softly and looked down at the blurry ripped paper. Poking out from between the pages she saw the corner of a photograph. Wiping her eyes with her sleeve, she tried to focus in on the face. His sandy brown hair and dark brown eyes looked straight into hers. His crooked grin made his happiness comical.

Beth was back in the middle school parking lot after school, standing in line to board a bus that would take them all to Mt. Mulholland, the closest ski hill. The cold hurt her face, sneaking past the scarf and giving her a ruddy, embarrassed look. Everyone in line hopped a little, trying to keep their feet warm enough so the ride on the school bus would be bearable. If they started with a chill, it was all over; they'd never warm up. Actually, they didn't look much different at the middle school parties, everyone jumping because they'd never really learned to dance. It was a lost art, like cursive writing or driving a stick shift.

Then he joined her in line, those dark brown eyes with one arched eyebrow that asked, "Sit with me?"

Her smile answered for her.

They settled into the seat, and he offered her a piece of strawberry bubble gum.

"Thanks, Scott," she said, "strawberry is my favorite. Well, real strawberries anyway."

"Who says these aren't real?"

"The label, the flavor, the lack of seeds. I could go on."

"Ha! Never mind. I'll keep it."

"No, really, I'd like it," she said. "I bet I can blow a bigger bubble than you."

"Not likely."

"There's a lot you don't know about me."

"I'm here to learn."

"Smooth. Okay, let's both blow bubbles with our heads against the back of the seat, and the first one to blow a bubble that touches the seat in front of us, wins."

"Sounds fair, gross, but fair, you first."

"Okay."

She blew a massive bubble that deflated before it even got halfway to the seat back. "I don't think we have enough gum for this game," she admitted.

"I didn't peg you for a quitter."

"Don't judge me. I have goals."

"Like—"

"Staying warm until we get there." He leaned against the window, making a soft cushion for her to lean back on with his parka. She leaned back, feeling warmer already. The driver had turned up the heat, and the moisture of all the breathing kids had condensed on the inside of the windows.

An hour later, the bus driver announced their arrival.

"Okay, kids! Everyone up and out! We're here."

Beth woke up and looked around confused. Scott woke up too, and tried to look around, but couldn't. "What's wrong?" Beth asked.

"My head – it's stuck."

"What? Oh, wow – It's not stuck, it's frozen to the window!"

Beth took off her gloves and used her fingernails to scratch and peel his frozen hair off the windowpane.

"That can't be good for your brain. Do you think you permanently froze some brain cells?"

"Likely. Protect me?"

"Let's do this," Beth said and grabbed Scott's hand and headed to the slopes.

*   *   *

On the slope of her pile of stuff, Beth cried even harder. The memory of that night reminded her of too many things. The freshly fallen snow had sparkled under the lights that night as they glided back and forth, sensing a beginning, a connection. The giddy preteen wonder of liking someone who likes you back. Sharing hot chocolate in the chalet. Cuddled up on the ride home.

Then, in the spring, the accident, the phone call, the tears. He was always looking for adventure. Until that day, he could always make her smile. It took two days for the divers to find him. Beth would never again chew on a piece of strawberry gum or ski. She would remain lost because no one was looking for her.

She still had the skis. Two pairs of Rossingnols. They were lost in the drifts of another room. He had taken the joy while she gathered up the heartache, planted herself in the middle of it, used it to keep her warm.

*   *   *

She leaned back against the headboard, wondering where she was going to go with all this stuff. She saw some half-full bins stacked three high on the floor next to the bed. Consolidating their contents into one, she started to fill the other two with the books and school papers that covered the bed. She took the Sharpie out of her pocket, labeled them "College papers" and restacked them. *She would head to the laundromat to wash the bedding both here and on the couch downstairs. She would sleep in her own bed tonight. She could do this.*

She gathered the bedding into a giant wad, wrapped it in the duvet to make it easier to carry, kicked things aside to make a path to the door, and pried it open.

*   *   *

She was a regular at the laundromat since her basement machines were now inaccessible with any size basket or bag. She ran through the Jimmy John's drive-thru, grabbed a Beach Club Unwich and parked in front of the Laund-o-rama. The bell rang as she pushed the door with her backside, her arms full of too much cotton print and breadless sandwich. She knew she looked ridiculous, but her laundry baskets had long ago been filled with her mother's evening gowns, and this was not a place where she felt the need to be invisible.

"Hey, Gwen," Beth said to the older woman, who was always crocheting in the same broken blue plastic chair by the door. She was raising her ten grandkids in a second-floor two-bedroom apartment with no balcony. If Beth were her, she would do laundry every day too.

"Hey," Gwen said, "can I give you a hand?"

"Could you just hold my sandwich, so I don't get mayonnaise on my laundry? That stuff never comes out."

"Sure."

Beth awkwardly bent backward to get the sandwich within Gwen's reach, so she didn't dump her yarn on the filthy floor. "Thanks."

She shoved her bedding into a giant washer that would fit it all at once, bought a package of detergent and fabric softener in adorable, tiny, one-use bottles, and went out to her car to fish some quarters out of the center console. As she walked past Gwen, she took her sandwich back. "How are the grandkids?"

"Oh, you know. They keep me busy. The oldest is driving now, so that's a big help. I feel more like a gramma, and a little less like a volunteer chauffeur."

Beth laughed. "How old is the youngest?"

"Two. She's a sweetie, though. No terrible twos when you're number ten. No one would tolerate it. Least of all me." She shrugged and went back to her crocheting.

"They are lucky to have you."

"I'm thankful I can keep them together. There is nothing like sibling love, no stronger bond. No one else knows what it's like to have grown up in your house. As adults, they'll need each other -- even though now they're at each other's throats."

Beth got a little teary and turned away.

"You okay, child?"

"Only child."

"I'm sorry. I didn't know."

"It's okay. You'd think by now I'd have gotten used to it, but you're right. I need a sibling, someone to understand, more now than I ever have. But there isn't anyone."

"You'll have to cultivate some sister-friendships. Choose your family. That's what they did on *Friends*. Seemed to work out. I read in *People Magazine* that they still hang out, even though the show is over."

"Is there no situation where *Friends* doesn't offer the answer?" Beth smiled.

"Nope."

"I'll have to dig out my DVD's. I think I have all ten seasons."

"Or just go find some sister-friends."

"Right." Beth thought about Kendra. Maybe a walk to DQ would be a step forward. Maybe she should call Adam. She needed fun too.

An hour and a half later, Beth gathered her clean linens into a newly fresh ball, put the two one-use bottles in her pocket, nodded to Gwen, and went home.

As she slammed the car door in the driveway, she could hear Goliath's little claws scratching to get out. *That dog and his tiny bladder.* She quickly opened the door, and he bound past her, out into the grass. Beth found the box in the front room labeled, Recycling. She put both tiny bottles in it and snapped the lid shut. While she didn't reduce, reuse, or bring anything to be recycled, at least she wasn't contributing to the landfills.

She made up her couch with the clean sheets and sat down, her feet up on the unicorn turned ottoman, and began to reread *The Boxcar Children*. Instead of comparing herself to them, as she had as a child, she tried to learn from them. She imagined their fear, their loneliness, their hardships. They were tough, resourceful, brave. They played the hand they had been dealt as best they could. Beth read about the flowers they had picked to place in a tin can vase on the rickety table of their boxcar and resolved to reclaim one whole room of her house. She needed a clear space to clear her head. If she was on this journey alone, she'd better pack.

That night she slept in her own bed, Goliath next to her, for the first time in months. She did worry a little about navigating to the bathroom at night, so she didn't drink anything for hours before bed, but she felt more positive than she had in a long time. Her trip to Chesapeake, the people she had met, the future she was imagining, it made her feel as though things would get better, that there was a kernel of hope in the corn maze of her life.

Chapter 9

If we all seized our heroic opportunities, the 6-o'clock news

would be a feel-good show.

Adam had just pulled into his driveway after work when his cell phone rang with an unfamiliar number. He answered anyway on a whim.

"Hello?"

"Hi, Adam? It's Bethany, from the shoe – parade – Ferris wheel, you know."

"Oh, hi! Did you need anything? Are you feeling okay?"

"Oh, yeah. I'm not looking for compensation or anything. I was just wondering, if – well – if you'd like to get together and do something this weekend? Maybe we could go to a cider mill or something? Pick apples and eat doughnuts? Climb a giant tower of hay bales? Feed farm animals from our hands? Does that sound like fun?"

"It does, actually. Since I live surrounded by so many orchards, they're easy to ignore. I don't think I've been to one in years."

"What's your favorite apple?"

"Honeycrisp has ruined me for all the other apples. I'm an apple snob."

"I bet they're even better right off the tree."

"I'll bet you're right."

"Saturday?"

"Sure."

"Um, Adam? I need to ask first. I don't want to be 'that woman' – the one that busts in on someone else's marriage. I really would just like to be friends. Will that be okay?"

"Of course. I could use a friend right now."

"Me too."

"See you Saturday."

"Bye."

After he hung up, he sat in his car for a while, wondering. He wondered if men and women could really be friends. He wondered if that was really what she wanted -- if it was what he wanted. He missed his wife fiercely, but with Dominique working out her issues elsewhere, he guessed this was the time to find out what it was he really wanted.

* * *

Windows down, Beth could hear the crackle as her Beetle rolled slowly over the gravel parking lot of Tree Top Cider Mill. She was shocked at how busy it was. She hadn't been to one since she was a kid on a field trip in elementary school, but that had probably been a weekday. Now it seemed that every family from a hundred miles around had the same idea. It was a perfect orchard day. The sun was out, and the temperatures were in the low 60s and getting warmer with a breeze that carried the smell of cinnamon doughnuts and apple cider right into her car window. She got out of the car, a blue knit infinity scarf tucked into the collar of her plaid flannel shirt, jeans, and a pair of tall yellow Hunter rain boots. The scarf made her eyes look even more blue. She looked a bit like a model on the cover of the L.L. Bean catalog, but she wanted to be comfortable, warm, and dry.

Not seeing Adam, she wandered into the shop and looked around. There were bags of apples and cardboard baskets of tomatoes and peaches on tables throughout the room. Against the walls, she saw shelves of canned preserves, honey, maple syrup. They were all from local growers with labels that looked like they'd been printed on someone's home computer, but she picked up some honey and some cherry preserves and got in line.

The line for the cashier was long. The family of seven in front of her had nine bags of apples, two dozen doughnuts in white boxes, and one of the younger kids was holding a shiny pumpkin with a funny face painted on it and a tuft of purple hair by the stem. One of the brothers, who looked like he was about twelve, was gesturing indiscreetly toward Beth and talking with his older sister. Beth couldn't hear everything he said, but she heard enough – parade… Mr. Connors…girlfriend.

She turned red, wanted to run. This was a small town. Everyone probably knew Adam; everyone had seen her run out into the street during the parade. Probably everyone had seen his wife's clothes all over the yard and knew about her big money boyfriend. She was in the middle of a scandal that had nothing to do with her, really. Accustomed to flying under the radar, she felt like she was in the glaring spotlight, instantly uncomfortable and sweating. She willed herself to stay in line and make her purchases, but then resolved to get to the car quickly and leave town. As she pushed open the heavy wooden door, a man reached out to hold it open for her.

"Adam, I have to go."

"What?! You just got here, right? Did I get the time wrong?"

"No, but people are talking about me, about us. I heard a teenager in line. It made me feel like I was on display, still in high school. That's not how I like to feel. I have to go."

"Wait, please." He stood between her and the parking lot. "This town is my home. These people all look out for each other. Because of that, sometimes they overstep. There are days when that is a good thing. They are watching out.

Sometimes it sucks -- they gossip-- make up their own conclusions. But it doesn't bother me. These are my people. Please stay."

"It will just get worse if they see us together here."

"Let me worry about that. Do you want to drop off that stuff in your car, so you don't have to carry it?

"Okay. But I didn't come here for drama."

"I hear you. Drama free. Promise."

They put the purchases in her car and walked to the back of the pavilion. The tractor waiting in the two-track was hooked up to a long hay wagon that was already almost full of people. She instinctively backed away from the crowd of rowdy kids and tired parents.

"Wanna walk?" Adam asked, eyebrows raised.

"Yes," she said, relieved.

They strolled, completely alone, down a row with Jonagold trees on their left and Macintosh on their right. The light was dappled, and the breeze was slowed by the rows of trees, so they just inhaled the scents of apples and campfire, and fresh dirt.

"Do you want to look for the Honeycrisps?" Beth asked.

"Sure. I think they put them on the ridge over there, prime real estate."

They hiked up the rolling hills together, past every kind of apple, past the entrance to the corn maze, past the pumpkin patch.

"You know I've never had a Honeycrisp apple. I always liked Granny Smiths."

"Well, allow me to introduce you. Honeycrisp, Bethany. Bethany, Honeycrisp." He picked a perfect apple from a high branch that the school kids couldn't reach and handed it to her with a flourish.

She bit into the red-green skin and was surprised by how crisp and sweet it was. It was just exactly how an apple was supposed to taste. She licked the apple juice off her lower lip and smiled. "You're right. One bite and I'm ruined."

"That was easy."

"This is too good. Can't fight it," Beth admitted, taking another bite.

"I didn't peg you for a quitter."

"No one does."

"I would like to grab a small pumpkin for my desk on the way back. Let's swing by the pumpkin patch."

"Okay. I could use a couple for my porch steps."

Their steps crunched through the dead pumpkin vines as they searched for the perfect ones. Weighed down with their choices, they made the long trek back to the pavilion, set their finds on an empty picnic table and walked over to watch the kids playing on the giant hill of hay.

The stairs were huge, made of gigantic rectangular hay bales stacked in what looked like a pyramid, but it was only half of one. The whole backside of it was a clear drop to the ground. They went around the back, wondering why the orchard hadn't made steps on all sides. Just then, a couple of boys that looked like brothers started to scuffle up above them. Beth's knees felt weak as she watched them. The bigger boy yelled, "I'm the king of the mountain!" while his mom snapped pictures on her phone. He raised his arms up and back, shoving his little brother backward off the top bale.

He fell fast, back first and kicking, as his brother and the other kids near the top looked on with horror, right into Beth's outstretched arms. The impact caused her to fall forward onto the hay-covered grass, but her elbows hit first and softened the impact for the little guy who looked up at her with wide eyes. His mother came around the corner of the hay bales at a speed no one would have thought her capable of. When she saw her little boy, safe in Beth's arms, she helped them up and hugged them both so fiercely that they almost squeaked.

"Oh my goodness, why isn't there a back staircase on this thing? Thank you – um --"

"Beth."

"Thank you, Beth. You are my hero." Then, noticing him for the first time, "Hello, Adam."

"Hello, Therese."

"Well, I better get these two hooligans home. I owe you, Beth. If you ever need anything. Adam knows where to find me."

"I appreciate that, but I'm fine. I am just happy I was here, and he's okay."

"Thank you so much." She scuttled her two disoriented boys down the wooden boardwalk and out of sight.

"Well, that was exciting! It looks like it was fate that you stayed. Now you're a local hero. I know Therese; this will be talked about. They'll forget me and you and the parade entirely."

"No, they won't."

"Can't we pretend?"

"You promised no drama."

"If you're going to go around being the Superintendent's kids' guardian angel, there isn't much I can do."

"Oh, geez, really? She's – your boss?"

"Afraid so, well, my boss's boss."

"Let's go for a drive. I'll put on my Audrey Hepburn sunglasses, so no one will recognize me."

"Deal. I'll drive."

*   *   *

As they sped down the country roads, the top off the Wrangler and the wind destroying her carefully styled hair, they talked and laughed and enjoyed the beautiful country houses, the perfect rows of corn, the ponds bordered with cattails and ducks floating around lazily. There was no one to notice them, and nothing to notice if they had.

"Where's your dog?"

"I brought him to his favorite kennel, Barkingham Palace. They treat him like a king there. I just wasn't sure what we'd be doing and if he'd be allowed everywhere."

"I bet they charge a fortune."

"They do, but it's worth it. I know he'll be happy until I get back."

"Well, in future, he can always come and stay with me. I have that fenced backyard, you know."

"Okay, cool, I'll do that, but only if you're sure that he can't wreck your beautiful furniture. Your house doesn't exactly look pet-friendly."

"Dogs are minimalists too. All they need is their human and food and a soft place to lie down, right?"

"True."

He slowed down and turned on his blinker before a small gravel lot.

"Mind if I pull into this park? The sun will be setting soon."

"Sure."

They faced a small lake, its shore dotted with cottages and rowboats pulled up onto the sand. Adam put his feet up on the dashboard and his hands behind his head and leaned back for the show. Beth followed suit.

"Are you glad you came?"

"Yes. Are you?"

"Of course! Now I don't have to worry and feel sad for my boss's boss's kid's broken neck."

"Well, I do save lives now and then."

"So it seems."

The sun had sunk low over the treetops across the lake, and Adam turned on the radio. They sat in silence. They didn't need to discuss this. The beauty spoke for itself. Their elbows rested on the center console so that their forearms touched. She moved away quickly, folding her hands in her lap. When it was over, and it started to get dark and chilly, she helped him hook the cloth top on the Jeep, and he drove her back to her car in the orchard parking lot and waved goodbye.

"Will I see you tomorrow?" he asked through the open car windows.

"I'll meet you at Beantown at nine?"

"Sounds good."

She nodded and headed back to Moira's B&B. Chesapeake was starting to feel like a second home, its people and places like old friends welcoming her back.

Beth could see Moira's soft silhouette making her bed through the turret room windows as she stood in the street. It looked like a scene from one of those John Hughes movies where the kids are out all night making bad choices and come back to the warm welcoming home they left, tired and ready for soup and a good talking to.

She knocked and waited. Moira's face in the door was so comforting that she almost cried. They hugged, and Moira led her into the parlor where there was already a fire burning and the two wingback chairs were ready with a bowl of popcorn and a bottle of Pellegrino, and two glasses filled with ice. Beth didn't even bother to go up to her room, but just dropped her bag in the foyer, kicked off her shoes, and cuddled up under a multicolored afghan all in 1970s colors, burnt orange, harvest gold, dark brown and avocado green.

"So, how have you been?"

"Oh, you know, just been doing. The garden club is slowing down for the season, and most of the activities and events that would draw in tourists to town are over, almost no one stays overnight to go to the orchard, so it's been pretty quiet. What about you?"

"Just working and running, cleaning up at my house a little, getting things ready for winter, mowing and covering my roses. You know, seasonal stuff."

"What did you need the bucket for? That you got here last time."

"Oh, that was for a little girl I met on my runs. I finally got to meet her mom. I think we might be friends. She's not a runner, but she seems kind, and she's about my age, so hopefully we'll have some stuff in common. Plus, we both think her daughter is pretty special."

"That sounds like a good beginning. Any gentleman callers? You seem like a catch."

"Ha ha, not really. I think I'm pretty used to my solitary life. It's not complicated, and I'm in charge. Well, sorta." Deflecting the subject, "What about you? You love love stories. Do you have one of your own?"

"A couple. Not recently, though. Back in the day, I could go out with any boy in the neighborhood. I am partial, as you know, to gray eyes, but I had my eyes on more than one handsome fella with a six pack of abs." The idea of this delighted her and made her lean back in the chair, satisfied, while she threw a handful of popcorn into her open mouth.

"What kind of a man was he? The one who really stole your heart? Can you tell me?"

"Oh, um, well, is this girl talk? It's been a while. Let's see. I was sixteen, and a naïve, little thing. His name was Jake. He was eighteen. He seemed so confident. He wanted to be a firefighter, so he knew he had to be strong and brave. He lifted weights with my older brother, Bill, in our garage every day after school. They were best friends and were planning to go to the firefighter training together. They used to play Led Zeppelin so loudly that the neighbors would complain. But my mom didn't mind. She loved that our house was where the kids hung out. She could keep an eye on everyone, make sure they were behaving themselves. She loved that her son wanted to be a hero. We all wanted that. Especially after my dad passed away and Bill was the man of the house."

"I'm so sorry."

"Thanks. It's forty-six or so years ago now, but I still miss him every day. I miss his rough, hardworking hands and the smell of his aftershave. Maybe I was looking to fill that hole, or maybe he just swept me off my feet, but I started watching them work out, and when he started watching me back, my heart fluttered. I was beyond smitten."

"Did your mom object?" Beth asked.

"It wasn't so unusual, back then, to have an older boyfriend. But when I realized that I was going to be having a baby, well, that threw me for a loop. I couldn't tell my mother; she'd be so disappointed. I couldn't tell Jake, because I was afraid he wouldn't stay. But it turned out that he didn't stay anyway. He went away to school that fall, and I didn't hear from him after that."

"Oh my goodness! What did you do?"

"I wore clothes to cover up my belly. I hid it, from everyone. And when she was born, four weeks early, in the upstairs bathroom at my mama's house, I wrapped her up in a blanket and gave her away. I knew I couldn't keep her, even if that's what I wanted to do most of all. I went to school the next day as if nothing had happened. I was empty."

"You poor thing. Do you know where she is now?"

"I do."

"Well, have you contacted her?"

"No. She won't want to see me. Not after what I did. There's no forgiving that."

"Those boys were trying to be strong and brave, but you were the real fighter. You were just a girl. You had the baby, all alone?"

"In the bathtub."

"I don't know what to say."

"It isn't really the love story you were looking for. Sorry about that."

"Oh, but it is. It helps me see you. Our stories bind us together."

"Tell me some of yours then."

Beth told Moira the story about Scott, her adolescent first love, and they both cried into their expensive water. "I used to love to ski. Now I can't even go near mountains. They will always ring with his laughter."

"Loss is a funny thing," Moira said. "It cripples and frees us."

"I don't feel free."

"Neither do I, but we are. There is nothing controlling us. We are able to be just who we are."

"I'm not sure I like who I am."

"I like you." They sipped their water and warmed their toes by the fire. When the popcorn was gone, they gave each other hugs and retired for the night.

*   *   *

As the sun rose the next morning, Beth was already out and running. She ran up the hill through the cemetery, where the asphalt path crisscrossed under trees that had been there longer than the town, longer than the residents lying at rest beneath them. The leaves quivered, but only enough to drop sprinklings of dew on her head and wake her to another day where she was strong and alive and breathing fresh air. She had been given the opportunity, again, to change her fate. As she ran through the high school parking lot, she saw kids with old rusty cars drag themselves to the natatorium for early morning swim practice. Soon they would be gliding through the cold chlorine, glad they'd made the effort, just as she was. There was pleasure in the exertion, to feel the strength in your calves and know that you could run fast and far, that you could probably outrun someone with bad intentions, that maybe you might outrun your own faults. This hope was fresh every morning, like a cup of tea from a new teabag, strong and hot, energizing and soothing.

She had meant to make a short, three-mile loop, but found herself running further, gaining stamina with each step. She saw a bridge over a narrow river, a stone stair leading down to a path along the riverbank. She usually didn't run on trails, but she couldn't stop. The leaves had started to turn colors, a little. Some reds and yellows were peeking through the green canopy and the river was percolating like a Sunday morning coffeepot after church. It made her spring forward, spurred by life. After a couple more miles, she stopped in a park up the river to check her pulse and assess her surroundings. There was a playground and a bandshell, a sand volleyball court and a frisbee golf course. Some college kids were playing; they looked like they'd been up all night. She remembered those days, when all she had to do was learn and play. She didn't have to do any work-study jobs like most of her peers, so she could spend many late nights and early mornings on swings and benches, walking through parks meant for children, talking until the wee hours about dreams and doubts, politics and religion, philosophy and biology. Giving up who you were just as you were becoming it. She wondered about those friends, the ones she never called back. The ones who sent their condolences when her parents died. The ones that hadn't seen past the front door of her house because she had wanted to see theirs. The ones who had received her "decline" RSVPs to their weddings and baby showers. The ones that used to be her family and that she thought had given up on her. But it was her that hadn't trusted them with her new circumstances. She had buried herself farther back into the rooms and walls and piles until she couldn't see them anymore. Until the things that they had cared about together were so muffled and faint that she could no longer hear them through the closed doors, closed blinds, the dust.

These young men throwing Frisbees in the morning glow took little notice of her in her reverie. They yelled Fore! and continued past her into the trees. She turned and made her way back down the path across the wet leaves and tree roots, while the water pushed her forward and her memories couldn't hold her back. It was like gravity, this pull back to town and what was growing familiar. She checked her phone as she ascended the stone steps back onto the bridge leading to the high school. At the top, she leaned against the railing and checked her phone. 8:45. She'd been running for over two hours. She was far from exhausted, but she had promised Adam she'd meet him at nine. There was no time to bathe or change. There would barely be time to make it to Beantown by then. She probably looked a mess, but headed toward town, determined to be on time, to not keep the future waiting any longer.

Adam sat at the long copper counter, a large black coffee in a real mug and a newspaper in his hands. As she pushed open the door, the bell rang, and he turned,

"Wow, you look… amazing," Adam said, gobsmacked.

"Don't be ironic."

"I'm not. You are positively radiant, the flushed cheeks, the glistening skin, it's well, it suits you."

"Well thank you, but you may not want to get too close, I'm afraid my aroma may not be as mesmerizing."

"Pheromones. Never a bad thing."

"You obviously have never taken a whiff of my laundry."

"Are you trying to scare me away? It won't work. I'm onto you."

"Onto what?" she asked, suspicious.

"I'm a counselor, remember? I can see you keeping your distance."

Beth waved to the barista and ordered a green tea with honey.

"What happened to the latte?" Adam asked, giving up on his previous line of questioning.

"I only drink coffee in the afternoon. Tea in the morning."

"Isn't that kind of backward? No offense meant, of course."

"Well, I used to sit on my dad's lap while he drank his morning coffee, and we did the crossword puzzle together." The sweat and the industrial air conditioning system had lowered her core temperature and a chill shot up her back and made her quiver. "The smell in the morning makes me want to cry."

"I'm sorry. Do you want to talk about it?"

"No, I'm okay." She picked up the teacup the barista had brought and put her hands around it in a mug-hug, warming them. "Warm tea and honey will soothe it."

"I wish that cure worked for me."

"You still have an open wound. I have a scar."

The barista came over.

"Hey, Tess, can I get a scone? Maybe carbs are my magical elixir. You want one?"

"No thank you. Do you have any plans for today?" Beth asked.

"It's such a beautiful day; I was thinking about lounging on the deck of my house and reading a bit. Did you bring anything to read? I have a small library if you need something. We can just relax and enjoy the autumn air. Does that sound like a plan?"

"Yes, actually, that sounds really nice. I love to curl up with a good book on my screened porch, but it's cool and breezy enough now that the bugs won't be out. I just need to go back to my room and wash up."

"Okay. Meet me at my place in an hour?" He took his scone in a paper to-go bag, held the door for her, and they walked out into the bright morning in opposite directions.

As she trudged up the hill to Moira's, her legs began to feel a bit like jelly, the fatigue of the long run and no breakfast catching up with her. She even had to stop once and lean against a lamp post to regain her balance and focus. Next time she would have to bring a banana or an apple with her. She should have gotten some at the orchard. Coffee shops weren't known for their healthy breakfast options.

Moira had read her mind. While she showered and dressed, the sweet lady had made her a steaming bowl of oatmeal with golden raisins, sliced apples, and a whole pot of tea. She even left Beth alone while she savored every bite, bustling around the kitchen, sweeping the area just under the cupboards, where dog hair would collect if she had one, but instead there were only crumbs and dust. Moira gathered it all into a pile in the middle of the wide-plank oak floor, then she got a tiny dustpan and broom to sweep it up and throw it away.

Beth thought absent-mindedly about how long it had been since she'd had a floor to sweep. At her house she'd need a bigger broom for the heap of dirt, dog hair, and dust. Goliath would probably charge through it like a little boy in an autumn leaf pile. He used to run laps around her living room, jumping up the stairs to the front room, looping back around. Now he mostly slept when he was inside and only ran when he was in the yard. Her life had limited his movement as well as her own. She seldom ran with him, as his little legs couldn't keep up with her long strides, and ten miles was probably too much for him, since he was seventy in dog years. Although, she had run a half-marathon once where a man who looked older than that had passed her in the final mile. He was long and lean, with skin like old leather. His silver hair was still thick, and his gait was steady. He looked so happy, like every step was a privilege. Of course, his legs weren't six inches long. She made a mental note to take Goliath to the dog park when she got home.

"Can you drop that bowl in the sink? Oatmeal is like cement if it dries," Moira said. She was on her hands and knees, scrubbing the baseboards with an old toothbrush.

"I can wash it."

"Nope, guests cannot do work. Company policy."

"What company?"

"Victorian B&B LLC."

"You're making that up."

Moira smiled, and Beth put her bowl in the sink full of soapy water, thanked Moira, and ran out, horsehead knocker banging behind her as she pulled the heavy old door tightly shut.

Beth had her antique store copy of *The Boxcar Children* on the passenger seat of her car, but she was curious to nose around in Adam's library, so she didn't bring it. To be perfectly honest, she also wasn't sure what he would think of her for reading an old children's book and didn't want to have a therapy session over the implications of her childhood tea sets.

So, empty-handed, she knocked at his perfect front door. He was there in a moment, showing her into the kitchen where there was still half a scone on a plain white plate. She looked around, taking it in. The bottom cabinets were forest green, the uppers were white, and the appliances were stainless steel. The granite countertops were white with green veining, and the backsplash was white subway tile. It looked like it should be on an HGTV episode of Renovation Nation.

"This kitchen is beautiful!" Beth gushed.

"Thanks, I did it myself. I love the muted colors. It lets me wake up slowly. My newspaper and black coffee blend right in."

"Do you do the crossword?"

"I do."

She felt a bit overwhelmed by her own emotions and tried to hide it by asking for some water, but he saw. He got a glass of water and led her into the library that was also a den. The leather furniture and smell of books instantly soothed her.

He even had one of those desk lamps with a green shade. It was classy. It was beautiful. It all was.

"Let me get together some blankets and some tea for you. Feel free to borrow any book that looks good."

Just the fact that he had a library recommended him highly, but there was nothing like looking through someone's books to get a real sense of who they were. The first bookcase looked like schoolbooks, on psychology, children's learning, emotional conditions. The second case was full of classics, Dickens, Austen, Tolstoy. Thick leather-bound volumes with gilded titles and un-cracked bindings. *Did he read them that carefully, or were they just for show?*

On the desk there was a copy of *The Count of Monte Cristo* with a leather bookmark about a third of the way in. She checked. The binding was perfect. He was careful. He didn't have many *things*. There was no clutter, but the things he had he treated with respect. If they were worthy to stay, maybe they were worthy to cherish.

The third case was full of more modern titles, *For Whom the Bell Tolls, The Lord of the Flies, Siddhartha.* It was so hard to choose. She went back to the second case and found a perfect copy of *Anna Karenina.* She hadn't read it for years, but longed to re-experience the story now, as an adult on her own. The first time she had read it was in college, her Russian

Literature class. She had remembered feeling Anna's passion, and Levin's joy, but not really understanding her loss. The book cradled in her arm, she wandered out to the back deck.

The yard was completely private, with a solid wood fence and tall shade trees around the perimeter. On the deck were two wooden lounge chairs with red cushions and a small folding table in between. Adam came out with blankets and tea, and Beth snuggled down into the chair, ready to spend a relaxing afternoon.

"*Anna Karenina.* Good choice. I have to grab my book – be right back."

When he returned, she was already engrossed. The first line has that effect on people: *All happy families are alike; each unhappy family is unhappy in its own way.* There certainly were a lot of ways to be unhappy. Were all happy families like Danny's? Were there always guitars and buckets full of dreams and polo on bikes? Were there always tall grasses, cracked sidewalks, and peeling paint? Or were they really unhappy, just in a different way? She would get to know them. She would find out their secret. If there was a formula, she would find it. She had been unhappy long enough.

Beth looked over at Adam, who was now in the Count's world. He smiled as he read about Edmond Dantes, the poor sailor and escaped convict that found the world's greatest treasure. The sailor's integrity was rewarded one-hundred-fold in the loyalty of his man, the vastness of his fortune, the scope of his power.

Feeling peaceful in the afternoon silence of the new backyard and the company of a new kindred spirit, Beth blinked away her astonishment at her day and her circumstances and read, sipped tea, breathed deeply. Every once in a while, she looked over at him. He didn't doze off; he didn't read over her shoulder. He remained fixated on the words in front of him, the world that Dumas created, the people that filled his dreams. Maybe he dreamed of the fortune that could have made Edmond's life easier. Maybe he wanted a beautiful woman like Mercedes to pine for. She really didn't know him yet. She was eager to. It had been a long time since she knew anyone, felt known.

Before long, she fell into Moscow's social season, the whirlwind of parties and snowy carriage rides, infidelity and reconciliation. The afternoon was a blink.

Caught up in the fictional drama, she was jolted out of her reverie by the thud of a giant walnut on the deck by her feet. Even Adam looked up. Then they watched as a pair of tiny black eyes peered through the slats of the railing. A squirrel with a long, bushy black tail came scampering across the wood planks, picking up the nut with its shockingly human hands and putting it in his teeth. It looked at them, froze. Eyes darting back and forth, it ran for the tree and was up on the lowest branch in a heartbeat, breathing in success and out fear. They watched it as intently as they had just watched the pages, a sciurid drama playing out before their eyes. The squirrel set the nut down on the branch and looked back at them. A breeze fluttered the leaves and the nut fell, softly and quietly, into the grass. The squirrel returned to the ground, intent on adding that nut to his winter store. Again, he dragged it up the tree trunk. Again, it fell. They watched this pattern repeat itself three or four times before the squirrel got the walnut into the hole in the tree trunk, and the spell was broken, and they sat, weirdly delighted, in the real world.

"How adorable was that?" Adam said.

"So adorable. I was rooting for that little guy."

"He was like Rudy."

"Right? He worked so hard, and winter's coming. We should surprise him with a basket of acorns. I have tons in my back yard from my neighbor's oak tree that hangs over my fence. I usually throw them away, but I could gather them for him."

That wasn't true. She had *many* plastic bins in her garage and shed full of the acorns of ten autumns. Her stores were enough to feed this squirrel for his whole life and probably all of his descendants'. She couldn't say that, of course. But maybe this could be a way to let go. Like the toddler who gives her pacifiers to the nursery at her day care because she doesn't need them anymore, but the babies do. She doesn't need them. *I don't need them. Of course, I don't. What on earth will I do with 20,000 acorns?* It was a question that never mattered before.

"Should I?"

"Why not? I'm sure he would appreciate your generosity. So-- you're coming back then? Not just to Chesapeake, but to see me, or at least my squirrel?"

"Yes. And to return your book, when I finish it."

"That could be awhile. How about you make two trips? Or I could come visit you?

"Um, no, I really enjoy getting out of the city. I'd rather come here if that's okay with you."

"Sure. Please bring Goliath, though. I feel a bit guilty asking you to keep coming all the way up here."

"It's really not a bother. One of the women I work with *lives* here! She does the drive every day. I think I can handle it on weekends."

"I have a guest room, if you'd rather not pay for lodging."

"Thanks, but no. I think Moira would be offended. She and I are getting to be quite good friends. Plus, you know."

"Drama?"

"Yep."

"I hear you."

"Thank you."

They sat there wrapped in their blankets, sipping their now-cold tea, willing time to slow down as it quickly got darker. Inertia was setting in. If she didn't get up soon, she'd end up sleeping on that deck.

"I really have to hit the road," Beth reluctantly admitted.

"I'll see you out. Please, keep the book as long as you'd like. My library doesn't collect fines."

"Let me help you clean up."

She gathered her cup and blanket and brought them into the living room, where she folded the blanket carefully.

"Where does this go?"

"Up in the linen closet. I can do it."

"No, let me help. Upstairs?"

"Here, I'll show you." Adam led her up to the closet in the hallway outside the room he had shared with his wife.

Beth peeked in as he made room for the quilt on the tidy shelves. It was sparse, just like the rest of the house. Impeccable. Clean lines, a bed neatly made, sheer curtains that billowed softly, chaise with a small quilt thrown over the arm. One that she swore she had seen before.

"All set?" Adam asked.

"Yes. Thank you again. It's been lovely."

"My pleasure."

They walked down the steps and through the house out into the driveway. She held the book tightly in her left arm, hugging it to keep it safe. He reached out, just as she turned away, caught her hand. It wasn't a handshake. More of a squeeze. She squeezed back. And walked away.

*　　*　　*

After a quick goodbye with Moira, she set out for home. It was already dark, and the dog kennel would be closed for pick-ups. It felt weird to be on a car ride without Goliath. The darkness and the cool wind made her feel invigorated, like riding a bike down an empty street at night. Freedom felt like that. She was invisible and invincible at the same time. Maybe her mother felt that way when she drove away from the house where Beth was a child, away from her dad, away from her things.

With only the clothes they had been wearing, they sped from the underground parking lot in her mother's new forest green BMW. The dried tears made Beth's cheeks stiff; they felt as if she showed any emotion, they would crack. She huddled in the back seat, invisible.

"Cherisse? Where are we going?"

"To my parents' to regroup."

"All the way to Traverse City? It's so far and late."

"But it's also where we will be welcomed without question. Loved without strings."

"Will Santa know where I've gone?"

"I let him know."

"Okay," Beth yawned. "Will you put on my lullabies?"

"Yes, Beatles?"

"Please, Cheri."

The four-hour car ride began with "Back in the U.S.S.R." played on a worn cassette tape, and Beth was sound asleep by "Ob-La-Di, Ob-La-Da." Cherisse knew these probably weren't considered lullabies by anyone else, but she found them comforting nevertheless. Children were comforted too, by familiar sounds and melodies; it really didn't matter if the song was written for them or not, and this way, Cherisse wasn't forced to listen to mind-numbing children's music. Instead, she could focus on remembering herself rocking her baby daughter to sleep in her powder pink nursery, swaying forward and back to the melody of "While My Guitar Gently Weeps." She could have hired someone for those exhausting *first years. She could have slept more, worked on her fragile marriage. No one would have blamed her. But she didn't. She sat in that rocker all night some nights. She needed to do this herself. She wouldn't quit. But -- persevering takes its toll. Some days it didn't seem worth it. And then, when her forehead was permanently creased, her hips widened, dark half-moons under her eyes, then it all fell apart. Then she was told that it wasn't working, that she wasn't loved like she thought, that a baby wouldn't fix anything, that sometimes you didn't get to choose whether you would quit.*

As Cheri fell deeper and deeper into her reverie, her eyelids drooped. She didn't want to wake Beth to stop for coffee. She had to keep the heater on to keep her warm. Cheri was cradled by the plush leather seats, the warm-moist air, the notes of the guitar, the soft breathing of her little girl. The cruise control and the long straight highway left her participation in the trip unnecessary.

When she opened her eyes, she saw the trees in front of her. She spun the wheel violently, swirling through the gravel of the soft shoulder, back up onto and across the highway. She shrieked, a high, unintelligible, pathetic noise that she had never made before. It woke little Beth, but the force of the spin left her little addled mind unaware of the circumstances until they squealed to a stop on the opposite side of the highway, inches from a steel Exit sign. They looked at each other. Saw no blood, no torn anything. Simultaneously, they burst into laughter. The relief of their safety, the release of their burdens, the camaraderie of their new relationship, it struck them then as beyond hilarious. They were still laughing when concerned drivers that had watched their spin with amazement, peering through the foggy glass of the car windows, knocked and asked if they were okay. Wondered if the giggling driver was drunk.

"That was a miracle, what just happened," said a man in a blue parka. "With all this holiday traffic, you slid through it like you were in <u>The Twilight Zone</u>. I've never seen anything like it."

Beth, thirty-some years later, on the same highway but going south, still felt that that night was a miracle, all of it. She and her mom had stopped at a truck stop after that and eaten strawberry shortcake Good Humor bars while they sat on a dirty bench. Cheri bought Beth a camouflage t-shirt, a Michigan magnet and two candy bars. They watched scruffy smiling truckers walk by, gassing up and drinking coffee from Styrofoam cups. They forgot for a minute that it was the beginning of everything being different. They forgot they were driving away from home. She even forgot to call her mother Cherisse and her mother forgot to correct her. They were just happy to be safe and together. They were in no hurry, because no one was expecting them where they were going or where they came from.

As Beth pulled into a truck stop with a diner attached, she decided she wasn't hungry, but rather wanted to look at all the kitschy souvenirs. She strolled down a narrow aisle that had badly tie-dyed t-shirts with various Michigan slogans on them, magnets in the shape of mittens, postcards of the sand dunes on Lake Michigan, even though they were literally hours away, die-cast American cars with shiny paint and complicated pin-striping. She bought one of each and a large coffee in a Styrofoam cup.

"Just visiting?" the cashier asked, looking at all her souvenirs in a pile on the counter.

"Nope. Lived here most of my life. I just like to have things that remind me of good days. Today was good."

"Okay then, to each their own." He rang up her order. "Drive safe."

"Thank you."

*   *   *

Arriving home, she found the most current bin labeled "Vacation souvenirs" on the bottom step of the staircase and put in her new memories. She got a glass of water from the kitchen sink and brought her bag and Adam's copy of *Anna Karenina,* carefully sidestepping magazines and dog toys, up the stairs to her bed. She made a mental note to pick up the magazines tomorrow; now that she was committed to coming upstairs every day, their slippery pages were a real hazard, and injury, for a runner, is an unwelcome option. How would she get crutches or a wheelchair through her pathways? She wouldn't. She laid the book on the spot where Goliath would normally sleep. It was 11:45 – too late to keep reading when she had work in the morning – so she set the alarm on her phone for 5:30 A.M., and instantly drifted off.

*   *   *

In the morning, she filled her hydration belt with water, laced up her running shoes on the screened porch and headed off on her usual route in the dark. She had decided to leave Goliath at the kennel until after work, so he would have another day of not being stuck alone in the house. It was chilly, so she started faster than normal and by 6:30 was sweating and warm, her sweatshirt tied around her waist, and the not quite yet a sunrise was beginning to make the horizon glow orange. At her midway point, it was the soft light of morning. She stopped in the cul-du-sac and checked her pulse. Normal. Then she heard a familiar screen door slam. She looked over and saw Kendra coming down the steps. She was wearing sweatpants and a baggy sweatshirt. On her feet were some old cross-trainers with bright pink laces.

"Would you like some company?"

"Of course, but I thought you didn't run."

"I don't, but I want to. Will you walk with me today? I can work up to it. I promise I'll walk really fast."

"Okay, that would be good for me too. I ran way too far yesterday. I could use a change of pace."

"Really?"

"Let's go."

They started at a steady walking pace, swinging their arms to match the pace of their legs. It felt good to have someone to be near. Someone who didn't know her, but maybe wanted to. Someone she admired, albeit from a distance, and wanted to be friends with. She started cautiously, with familiar common ground.

"Is Danny's new bucket list working out?"

"Oh, it is! She loves having so much room for her dreams. I love her optimism. She seems to smile through everything, even struggles."

"She always seems to be having fun when I see her outside, building or playing or exploring."

"Danny is an only child, and only children tend to have such amazing imaginations, or so I've read. And if Danny is any kind of example, well, when she was little, she had an imaginary friend named Sue. Sue was a purple octopus that loved to sing in a high voice and needed good acoustics for her concerts. So, she lived in the bathtub that Danny kept filled with water. Every now and then I'd be missing my saltshaker, and I'd find it on the edge of the bathtub. She would tell me that octopi lived in salt water and anyway salt would give us all high blood pressure."

"Ha ha! What a clever little one. I was an only child too, but I don't think I dealt with the loneliness in such productive and interesting ways. Instead, I imagined dark and scary possibilities. That may have to do with my parents splitting when I was so young, though. Or maybe I'm just a melancholy soul."

"I'm so sorry. Divorce is so hard, but when kiddos are little sometimes I think it shapes their whole world view."

"Yeah, I wish I had been stronger, hadn't let it shape me quite so much."

They passed the Dairy Queen, closed now, and headed up and over the highway overpass. They stopped at the top and looked down over all the cars on the serpentine strips of concrete. They were cruising along at posted speeds, oblivious to the people above them, but Beth and Kendra could feel the whoosh of each one going past. It was like the cars were trying to suck them into the vortex of modern life, where there is no time to stop and feel the pull, like gravity, toward activity and busy-ness. The eternal multi-tasking and bragging about being the most harried person in the conversation. The family meals where no one has time to attend. The grocery shopping done via the internet and picked up at the curb because there's no time to go inside because you may run into, and have to talk to, your neighbors.

They stood quietly, feeling the pull.

"You seem pretty strong to me," Kendra said.

"Only physically. My running is an escape mechanism, avoidance really. Inside, I'm a hot mess."

"We all are."

"No, you're not. You have your priorities all straight. I admire your family so much. That sounds creepy, probably. But I've run past your house every day for years. There is always music, and laughter, and little girls on bikes."

"It's not as perfect as it may seem."

"Are you unhappy? Sorry, that's probably none of my business. Definitely none of my business."

"It's okay. I'm all about transparency. If we're going to be friends, let's be real. I am not unhappy. But I'm exhausted. I am the sole provider for the family, plus taking care of Danny and my husband. Well, sometimes it's more than I can handle with any grace."

"Is your husband okay? I assume you mean more than picking up socks and gathering coffee cups from every flat surface."

Kendra paused. Her eyes got watery. "Jackson, my husband, was diagnosed with ALS five years ago. His muscles have been deteriorating since before then. He hasn't been able to work for years; he was in construction. He certainly can't be up on a roof. Now, he can't even play his guitar." She slumped against the fence, "I'm so sad for him."

"I am so sorry, but didn't I hear guitar music just last week?"

"You probably did. He made Danny and me an instrumental CD of his songs when he was first diagnosed so that we could still sing together when he couldn't play."

"That is the sweetest thing I've ever heard. Why does everyone have to be fighting such a profound battle? I don't think I've ever met anyone that was free from it. Some just cope better?"

"Or they're just really good actors. I would have never guessed that you carry any baggage."

"That story is probably too long for this walk. I have to head for work here soon, so maybe we should head back?" Beth asked.

"Sure."

"I promise I'm not dodging the question." Beth said quickly, "I think it will probably be really freeing to voice it. I just don't want to rush. Is that okay?"

"Of course," Kendra replied, "it's your story to tell, how and when you want. Or not at all. But I'm here if you want to. If you think it will help."

"I really appreciate that. I... am not an open book. I lean toward opaque. But I'm working on it. And for what it's worth, I am so sorry about your husband's illness. I will be keeping all three of you in my prayers."

"If you'd like to meet Jackson, maybe you could come with us to DQ tonight? It's an end-of-summer tradition for us. It will be closing for the season in a week or two."

"I'd love to."

"Great, let's put our numbers in each other's phones so we can keep in touch."

They exchanged phones and added themselves to each other's contact lists. Beth was shocked when she saw the time.

"I'm gonna be pushing it. Talk to you soon!" and she ran off toward the west side of town at a breakneck pace.

Kendra, on the other hand, meandered back through several subdivisions, in no hurry at all. Jackson said he would make sure Danny got on the bus, and the rest of the afternoon was hers to sleep and tend to her husband. Her night shift at the hospital had just ended when she came out to meet Beth, so she was in the midst of her third shift *evening* as everyone else was heading to work. The long hours of caring for patients and her family had isolated her, so making friends and keeping them had been difficult. She was hopeful that she and Beth would be friends. It is so difficult in the late 30s and 40s to find meaningful friendships. It is harder to overlook flaws than it was in school or even the unpredictable 20s. Now people needed to fit into her life more precisely. Like a beautiful bridesmaid's dress in a full closet. There was no extra room, but the need was still there. Sometimes it was even stronger. No one reminds a woman of who she really is like a close girlfriend. They are the only ones that can shush, compliment, or tell her she's full of crap and be listened to and believed. They are the touchstones of womanhood. Childhood friends are the best, but in their absence, a new, sincere friend can fill that gap.

Neither woman was under any illusions that their salve would be found, but this looked promising. They were willing to give it a shot.

*   *   *

That evening, Beth drove over to the kennel to reunite with her furry companion. When she walked into the big canine *living room,* twenty dogs turned their heads from the

Puppy Channel to see who had joined them. Only one, little Goliath, jumped down from the arm of the big red sofa, wagging furiously and rubbing up against her legs. She scooped him up and let him kiss her neck with his tiny tongue while she scratched his belly and laughed, thankful to be once again loved without question. He wriggled and seemed to smile up at her.

"Come on, we're going to DQ with some new friends." The lilt in her voice seemed to energize him, so much so that it felt as though he wasn't just hearing her, but *hearing* her. He slid down her forearm and into her handbag, peeking out at her, tongue lolling. On the front seat, Goliath climbed out and put his little paws on the door armrest. One of his feet hit the window button. His eyes got even wider as the wind started blowing through the car, crisp and clean. He scooched up and rested his tiny chin on the edge of the window and let the wind push him backward against the seat. He was with his person and totally content.

Beth and Kendra's texts throughout the day had led to the decision that they would have hot dogs and ice cream for dinner to celebrate the end of summer and the beginning of their friendship. Beth was excited to meet Jackson and was a little curious to see what kind of ice cream Danny would order. What flavor was all the rage today? When she was little, there was nothing like a big waffle cone full of Blue Moon. It stained her lips blue and made her look cold, even on a hot summer day. No sprinkles, just creamy blueness, the color her mother would have painted her baby brother's room if she'd had one.

"Hey! Glad you could make it," Kendra called out across the parking lot as she maneuvered her husband's wheelchair out of the trunk and helped him into it. He could still push up a little with his legs, so he helped as much as he could. Beth stood back, mouth open in admiration, too surprised to remember that she could be helpful. Once he got situated, Jackson looked up and introduced himself.

"Nice to meet you. I'm Jackson."

"Likewise. I'm Beth."

"So, I hear you're inspiring my favorite ladies."

"Excuse me? Me?"

"My wife is exercising; my daughter is playing polo and collecting dreams in cool old buckets."

"Maybe I exercised with your wife, but your daughter is completely responsible for all her own big dreams, including the polo. I've never even seen a match. Although I did get in the way of her trusty Schwinn once on a run. Does that count?"

"You seem to have made an impression."

"Well, I'm flattered. Especially since I admire them both so much. You too, to tell you the truth. I've heard you sing as I run by. Your voice is lovely."

"Does it really carry out onto the sidewalk?"

"It does."

"Next time I'll try harder knowing I may have an auxiliary audience." He smiled crookedly. "Well, who's ready for ice cream?"

"Me!" Danny yelled from the metal railing she'd been swinging from.

Kendra wheeled Jackson's chair up the cement ramp, and Beth had the wherewithal to hold the door. Danny was already inside trying to decide what to get, not that there was really ever any question. They stood in silence for a minute looking at the extensive menu of stickers on the window.

Out on the picnic table beside the building, under two massive maple trees, they spread out their feast. They had hot dogs, French fries, and soon the teenager inside would be bringing out their ice cream. Kendra took a little packet of plastic silverware out of her purse and cut Jackson's hot dog into tiny pieces, then cut the fries into thirds. Beth watched with curiosity and awe, while eating a bite or two, but leaving the majority of her food uneaten. Danny took the hot dog out of the bun, cut it into chunks and dipped each one in a giant blob of ketchup. When the ice cream came, the hot food was forgotten. Danny's cake batter with sprinkles in a waffle cone looked like a colorful celebration. Kendra and Jackson shared a bowl of chocolate and vanilla swirl soft serve. Kendra slowly served him small spoonfuls that he rolled around in his mouth, savoring. Every once in a while, she would give herself a taste, but she seemed to do it only to validate that they were *sharing*. There was no relish. Maybe she didn't want to negate their earlier exercise. Maybe the flavors weren't her favorite, but his. Beth wondered and marveled at their comfort with each other, their dedication, her patience. It was beautiful. She lingered over her baby cone of butter pecan as the sun set over the rooftops of the old houses that lined the narrow street.

"Sunrise and set together today, huh?"

"Am I crowding you?" Kendra asked.

"What? I'm the one who invaded *your* lives. I'm just happy to be here with your sweet family."

Danny had finished her dessert and was petting Goliath with sticky fingers, then picking the stray dog hair out from between them. She didn't even seem to notice the little attentions her mother paid her father. Her foundations were secure and above question.

Chapter 10

The pain and joy of starting over is a blessing and a torment.

Dominique sat on the edge of the bed in the motel room at the edge of town. It smelled like cat pee and the ugly Berber carpet was faintly sticky, so she was afraid to remove her shoes. She sat rigid. She needed to get her head together.

The night before she and Adam got married, she had stood in the street outside his parents' house in the city and looked up at the one lit window, wondering if now was the time to tell him everything. She had tried to only let him see who she had become and not saddle him with her baggage. But then it seemed too late. She would have seemed deceitful if she told him then. Then had not been the time. Later. She had walked away.

Ten years later, the right moment had never arrived. And here she sat, alone with her guilt and feelings of inadequacy. She couldn't tell him now. She looked back at the scratchy quilted duvet in a garish green pattern, wondered if it had been washed, and couldn't even flop back into her hopelessness. There was no soft, clean, safe place to fall. She looked at the nightstand. A cheap digital clock blinked 12:00.

The thick curtains kept the room dark. If time was passing, she was unaware of it. She twisted her wedding ring around her finger. There was no sparkle.

*   *   *

Beth and Goliath arrived on Adam's doorstep that Friday evening freshly groomed. Goliath had just been washed and his nails trimmed at Barkingham Palace. Beth had gotten her hair done and was wearing a sleek black dress with a red chiffon scarf.

"Well, hello!" Adam swung the door wide. "You both look amazing." He knelt down to scratch Goliath's head as the dog instinctively ducked behind Beth's legs.

"He's a little shy at first. We don't have many outings like this. Or we haven't, in the past. Seems as though it will get to be a regular thing, though. Thank you so much for letting him stay at your house while we go out. Moira has other guests this weekend and wasn't sure if she'd be able to keep him there."

"It's fine. Relax. This house has very little that can be ruined, and he seems so well behaved."

"Oh, he is! Okay, well, are you ready? I'm so excited! I haven't been to a concert in ages. I resisted the urge to look up who was performing this weekend, so I could be surprised. But tell me. I can't stand it."

"Adele ring a bell?"

Beth screeched. She never would have guessed. *Such a big ticket. On such short notice. These tickets hadn't been bought with her in mind. They sold out six months ago.* She sobered, tried to concentrate on facts rather than feelings.

"So which venue? She doesn't seem like a Pine Knob, outdoor concert, kind of performer. And I'm not dressed for the outdoors."

"The Palace, you're perfect. They're not great seats, but with a voice like that, I bet it will fill the whole place."

"Let me get Goliath settled, and we can head out." She grabbed his bag from the car, set up food and water and a cushion on the floor between the couch and window, by the heat vent in the floor. "Be good, Buddy. I'll be back after a while." She gave his head a pat.

"You driving?" Beth asked.

"Up to you. Do you want to?"

"Actually, yeah. You should be able to assess my driving like I did yours."

"I was under evaluation?"

"Of course. Every little thing tells me something. I know that you love fun, wind in your face, you are considerate of other drivers, keep your passengers safe."

"I hope I have a similar list for you later."

"Don't hold your breath."

"Uh Oh."

They slid into the low seats of the Beetle; Adam noticing first the little bud vase on the dash, with a beautiful blue silk hydrangea. He noticed the massive head room created by the domed roof, and the two giant plastic tubs in the back seat. "What's in the tubs? You staying a while?"

"Acorns. For the squirrel."

"That must be a big tree your neighbors have."

"It is."

They headed down the road, Beth barely pausing at the stop sign before turning onto the two-lane highway out of town.

*   *   *

Dominique decided, there in the nasty old, rented room, that she would tell him everything. She would come clean not because it was time to tell the truth, but because it was long past time. He didn't understand her at all. He saw her cheekbones so delicate, graceful wrists and ankles, heard her soft voice, intelligent conversation, but he only knew who she allowed him to see. Through no fault of his own, his information was incomplete.

After driving around the block a few times, she pulled up in front of his house, their house. She pulled into the driveway behind his Jeep. She parked and sat. *Had she given him enough time? Would he open the door? Had he already moved on?* She couldn't marinate on these questions for too long. She walked slowly up to the side door. Knocked. No one answered. Now was the time. She felt it. She had to talk to him tonight. She had to try and sew shut this wound with sutures of truth. She got her house key from her handbag, unlocked the door. She pushed it open with trepidation, not knowing if he was sleeping or watching T.V. or deliberately ignoring her presence. Her sandals made a thwacking sound on the tile as she came down the hall to the kitchen. The counters were empty, clean to the point of being sterile. No stray shredded cheese or bread crumbs, no pile of guilty garments on the table. No sign that anyone lived here at all. She fought the urge to make a bit of a mess, leave a knife smeared with peanut butter half-poised over the pristine steel of the sink.

She wandered through the house, room by room. There were only two things that stood out. In the living room she saw a dog bed and bowls. *Had he gotten a dog? Was he on a walk with it right now?* It was odd. He'd never expressed the desire for a pet. Then, upstairs, she went into their room and was met by a flood of emotion. His side of the bed was unmade. She could see the imprint of his body in the sheets. Fetal. He usually sprawled. This was not what she had wanted. She hadn't meant to break him. But the thing that really did it, the thing she would not be able to un-see, was the small bright quilt that stood out from the white sheets. Had her childhood comfort been comforting him? He had obviously slept with it, maybe breathing it in. Maybe thinking of her. Maybe remembering them together in easier times. The way her white dress and veil had contrasted with the green grass of the park lawn, the way they hadn't seen anyone but each other. She couldn't face those memories. Not when her heart was about to burst with the distant past she wanted to share and couldn't. He wasn't here. She would look for him. If he was walking a dog, he wouldn't be far.

She grabbed her blanket, ran out the door, threw it in her car and started driving down every street in Chesapeake, looking for her husband, the man who had tried to give her everything.

*   *   *

Goliath, waking up from his nap on the guest room bed, trotted downstairs to survey his surroundings. He took a couple sips of his water, ate a piece of tiny kibble, then noticed that the side door was open. He ran toward it, excited to go outside. On the stoop, he went into sentry mode as he'd been taught. He had a pretty good vantage point of the sloping yard from the top step, so he stayed and looked. Nothing glaring, shiny, messy. He sat, licked his front paws, but came to attention when he heard a car come down the street. It was long and sleek and black, moving steadily, close to the opposite curb. Just as Goliath was about to go back to licking, something brown flew out of the back seat into the yard. It looked like a stick. They were playing fetch! He bound across the grass to pick it up, but by the time he got to it, the car was gone.

Curtis, the soon-to-be groom in the back of the limo that day, was celebrating his bachelor party. His buddies were congratulating him on finding such a smart, beautiful, kind, accomplished bride. They were happy for him, excited for a night out on the town. They brought all kinds of celebratory memorabilia. A baseball hat with the word GROOM embroidered on it, drinks, smokes, laughs.

Curtis was not much of a partier. He preferred a quiet night in with his fiancé, Jenna. But this night was going to be epic, so he drank the drinks they gave him, put on the dorky hat, lit the cigar they offered him and took a long breath in. Then he choked, coughed, almost puked. His boys laughed at him, and when they turned their heads to shout music requests to the limo driver, he flicked that cigar right out the window, hard. It landed in Adam's yard and was quickly snatched up in Goliath's teeth as the limo drove away.

Carrying the *stick* proudly between his teeth, Goliath ran for the house and the box just inside the door. He deposited the litter in the box and sat waiting for his treat. No one came.

Since it appeared that no treat was forthcoming, Goliath made himself comfortable on the living room couch and waited for Beth.

*   *   *

Beth was not thinking about Goliath. She was lost in the beautiful music that filled the arena. Adele's black sparkling evening gown was barely visible from the balcony, but the screens broadcasted the whole concert as if you were right on stage with her. Her giant doe eyes opening as she sang, "Hello." She hit every note. She was a talent like Beth had never seen in person. Then she moved to the stage in the center, close enough to watch her lips move. She told stories in between her songs about her childhood, motherhood, fashion. She was so candid, so funny, Beth decided that if they ever met in person, they might be best friends. Adam even appeared to be enjoying it. "Are you a musical connoisseur?" Beth whispered loudly.

"I mostly listen to songs that soothe, classical stuff. This seems kind of like that, just with vocals instead of instruments. But, of course, I like all kinds of music, depending on my mood, the environment I'm in."

The concert had paused for a moment while Adele shifted back to the original stage.

"What would your dream concert be?"

"What artist? Um, --" His phone buzzed in his pocket. "Just a sec."

He took out his phone and looked at the glowing screen. "I just got a text from my neighbor across the street. There's an emergency. We have to go. Now."

"What!? Did he say what?"

"No. Just to get back ASAP. I trust him. He wouldn't overreact."

"Let's go, then."

They gathered their things and headed for the door. Beth looking longingly at the lights and the stage, then at the long tables of t-shirts, hats, and stickers as they quickly made their way down the circular concourse to the wide stairs that led to the parking lot. She still had her ticket stub. That would have to do as a souvenir.

They ran across the massive parking lot; Beth had taken off her heels and was carrying them under her arm, clutching her purse in her other hand. They jumped into the Beetle and sped off toward Chesapeake.

There was silence in the car. Tense. Brittle. Adam brought his knees up to his chin. Beth gripped the steering wheel so tightly that her turns were jerky, jarring. Adam had to hold his knees with one arm and the armrest with the other to keep from tipping over. They both breathed slowly and deliberately. Trying to calm their inner terror. She drove as fast as she felt she could without risking a ticket. Adam tried to will her to go faster. Her phone buzzed. They both disregarded it. As they came over the crest of the hill above town, they could see the smoke rising through the cemetery trees. They turned down Adam's street to see emergency vehicles with flashing lights, neighbors standing on the sidewalk, gaping. Smoke billowing out the French doors of the balcony and the side door by the garage. A long spray of fire hose water was already soaking the roof and running down the walls. The red paint on the arched front door was blistering and bubbling with the intense heat. Firefighters valiantly ran from task to task, doing their best to control the flames and keep them from the garage and neighboring houses. When the neighbors saw Adam drive up, they ran to him.

"Was anyone inside?" James Harper, his neighbor that had texted, asked.

"Not that I know of," was Adam's reply.

"Goliath!" Beth shouted from behind him.

"Oh, yeah, her dog, Goliath, but no people," Adam agreed.

The firefighters were there now too, gathering information.

"We've been inside. We didn't see any animals or people."

"Maybe he's scared and hiding," yelled Beth, heading for the house.

"No, ma'am, we can't let you go inside. Was he wearing a tag? A license?"

"Of course."

"Please, check your phone. Maybe someone found him."

"But he couldn't get out! We shut the door when we left," Beth pleaded.

"It was open when we arrived, ma'am. I'd wager he's out."

Beth remembered the buzzing her phone made on the way home and ran to the car to retrieve it. She frantically entered her passcode and saw four texts, all from Moira.

Moira: Goliath missed me, I guess.

Moira: Found his way here.

Moira: He's safe with me.

Moira: Enjoy your concert.

Beth sat right down in the grass by the curb and sobbed with relief. Many times she had imagined this very scene. The flames licking up the siding, bursting windows, smoke and water, and devastation. But she had always imagined she'd be sitting in her own front yard, watching it all burn. Decades of family heirlooms, ensembles, condiment packets, souvenirs, collections, boxes of old running shoes, acorns. All gone. Here it was different. It wasn't her burdens being eliminated, but his carefully crafted and culled collection of modern furniture, his simple clothes, his books. This was all wrong. Adam came over and rubbed her back.

"Is he okay?"

"Yeah, Moira has him. I'm so sorry, Adam, your beautiful house."

"I'm not processing it all quite yet, but I had a sense that everything was going to be different now. That my former life is in ashes. I assumed it wouldn't be literal, but here we are."

"It kind of looks like they Set Fire to the Rain," Beth said sheepishly. "Too soon?"

They both looked up as the smoke, flames, and gush of the hoses made an unusual elemental collage against the evening sky.

"I'm so sorry," she said again.

"Not your fault."

The ashes rained down on their heads as they sat there. There was no wind, so they floated, delicately landing on eyelashes and shoulders, like an early December snowfall, when everything is peaceful, and the air hasn't yet turned bitter. The kind of snowfall in every Hallmark Christmas movie. But this wasn't pure and clean. It was the fallout of a devastated family. A house that had not been a home. An accidental catastrophe.

Beth had been alone for so long that she was clumsy in her comforting, hesitant to say anything at all. They sat in silence for a long time, backs to the house that had given them both a place to escape to.

*　　*　　*

It couldn't be saved. Not one stick of it. By nightfall, the upstairs had fallen into the basement, and it looked like a giant smoldering fire pit.

"I am going to run to Moira's and check on Goliath. I'll get you a room too. You're going to need a place to sleep tonight."

"Sure, thanks. Let the firefighters know. In case they need to reach you. Will you come back here tonight?"

"Should I? I feel kind of useless."

"You don't need to. I'll stay until they are done, then I'll join you at the B&B, okay?"

"Okay... It will be all right."

"Yeah, I have insurance. It's just stuff, right? And not much stuff really. It's not the loss of that really, but it feels like the end of something important. I tried so hard to make it stunning--"

"It was!"

"I wanted her to be proud of it, of us."

Beth didn't know what to say to that, how to defend a woman she'd never met.

"See you later?" she finally asked.

"Yeah."

Minutes after Beth's Beetle rounded the corner toward Moira's, Adam looked up again to see Dominique's Taurus headed toward him. What could he say to her? He had been out with another woman when their house had burned down. He hadn't been here to fix it. He was distraught thinking about the confession he would have to make. He had done this. It was his fault. He steeled himself for the conversation that loomed in front of him. He stood.

Dom looked at him, smoking hole in the ground behind him, and started to cry.

"I'm so sorry. This is my fault," she cried.

Adam tried to knock loose his confusion by shaking his head back and forth, "What? You? I don't understand."

"I came here to talk to you. I looked all through the house. I couldn't find you. I ran out and left the door open. I drove by later, saw it on fire, emergency was already here. I felt so guilty that I took off back to the motel, figured I'd let the fire people handle it. But I couldn't take it. Sitting there. I don't know what happened, but I did it. I'm sure. It was me." She fell onto the grass on her knees, weeping for the house and for all the mistakes she'd made. "I'll go. I just wanted you to know. I just wanted to say I'm sorry."

"You're living in a motel?"

"Yeah, the one over by Brenner's liquor store."

"Why?"

"Because I needed to be alone. To think. To suffer."

"Dom, your shoes are worth more than that motel. Come with me and stay at the B&B over on Maple."

"No. I don't deserve it. I'll be fine. I need time. So do you. She's probably waiting for you."

"Excuse me?"

"The woman with the dog. Or did you get a dog?"

"Dom, we're just friends."

"Okay."

It was dark now, and the glow from their basement was eerie. The yellow caution tape was whipping in the wind.

"Let's talk soon. I have to figure some things out, starting with where to live. You're not going to stay in that motel?" Adam asked hopefully.

"I have to figure some things out too."

"Let me know if you need anything."

"I will."

After his wife left, Adam sat on the cement steps that used to lead to his front door. Now they were a stairway to nowhere. His back was warmed by the heat emanating from below. He wondered how he got here. *What choices had led to this moment? They had always left a trail of devastation in their wake it seemed. Only a couple years ago, they had stayed in a log cabin in Gatlinburg, Tennessee. It was at the top of the mountain, the mist billowing all around them in the mornings. They had sat on the front porch every morning, steaming cups of coffee in their hands, looking out into forever. They had seen black bears playing in the woods. They had held hands as they walked the trails beside rocky rivers and past old logging lodges. They had posed beside waterfalls, held each other tightly as they hiked inclines with signs warning of dangerous falling rock, steep cliffs with no railings. They had had a wonderful time and returned unscathed. Then only months later, on the news, they saw the whole place go up in flames. He had no idea if that cabin was even still there, and if it was, if the two of them would ever see it again. Probably not. Either the cabin hadn't made it, or they wouldn't. Somewhere, something was always smoldering.*

He got up slowly, as if he was in pain, even though he physically felt fine. He decided to walk down to Maple Street, leave his Jeep in the driveway. The cool Autumn night air enveloped him, and he disappeared down the hill into the darkness, taking the long way around.

At about 11, he dropped the bit of the horsehead knocker as he stood on Moira's front porch. It made a satisfying clack. Moira bustled to the front door to let him in, pulled him in, hugged him.

"I'm sorry. Do I know you?" He tried to be polite, but he was not a hugger.

"No, but -- well -- um -- Beth told me what happened. I'm so sorry. Adam, is it?"

"Yes. Nice to meet you. Thank you so much for letting me stay. There is definitely a shortage of warm and welcoming accommodations in Chesapeake, and I really didn't want to drive into the city tonight."

"I am so glad I had an available room. Beth moved into it, so you can have the best one. The turret."

"That's not necessary."

"Oh, but it is. Beth insisted. She said that room would restore you like it did her."

"Well, thank you."

"Now come sit by the fire -- oh, well maybe that won't be comforting -- the dining room maybe? We can share some hot chocolate?"

"Could I take mine to go? Upstairs, I mean. Today has been really long; I'd just like to lie down."

Just then Beth and Goliath came swooping down the staircase.

"How is it?" Beth asked.

"The same."

"Let me show you your room; I'll bet you're tired."

He let her lead him up the curving stairs with their busy wallpaper and knick knacks. Everything was cluttered with old things and smelled of talcum powder and furniture polish. While it wasn't quite his cup of tea, he could appreciate that this would be preferable to a grimy motel in the shade of a liquor store and was thankful to be here. The cozy little round room at the top of the stairs was quaint, and the bed was soft and the pillows fluffy. He couldn't wait to snuggle in.

"I ran to the grocery store while you stayed at the house and got you some seasonal jammies. Sorry, they don't really seem like your style, but it's all they had. I got myself a pair too. Mine have black cats." She handed him a pair of orange fleece pajama pants with witches on brooms flying across them and a v-neck t-shirt with a witch hat in the middle.

166

"I don't have any clothes but these," he said, the impact of what had happened settling on him like a heavy blanket. Then he stared silently ahead. Shaking himself back to Earth, he asked, "Is Goliath okay?"

"Yes, well, I inspected him thoroughly when I got here earlier, and I found something. –Goliath! Come here. -- See?" She pointed to a round burn mark on his shoulder, a circle of ash. "Smell it."

"What? Why?" But he bent down over the little dog and sniffed. There was no mistaking the spicy sweet scent of a cheap cigar. "What does this mean?"

"Did the officers tell you where they think the fire started?"

"They said it was too early, but that they thought it started by the side door."

"Is there anything there? I don't remember."

"Just a recycle bin."

"Well, we can talk about it in the morning. I just wanted you to have any information I found. Good night. Thank you for the concert."

"You're welcome. Sorry we couldn't stay till the end."

"I'm sorry too."

After she left, he changed into the ridiculous pajamas and got into bed without any of his normal ritual. He would have fallen asleep immediately, but he lay there shivering - wishing she'd gotten fuzzy Halloween socks too. The house was drafty, and the fireplace had probably fooled the thermostat into thinking it was warmer than it was. Upstairs it was only a solid 61 degrees, and he just couldn't lose the chill after being out in the night air for so long. He was probably coming down with something. Finally, he got up, turned on the light, and started looking in the bureau for extra blankets.

He was on his hands and knees on the floor in front of the bureau when he saw *her*. There, on faded newsprint glued to the bottom of the empty drawer, was a beautiful girl he would recognize anywhere. Dominique, before she took his name. Between her parents, his in-laws, Anne and the late John Whittingham.

Chapter 11

Sometimes all we need is for someone to see us. There is nothing

like feeling seen in the middle of a Tuesday.

When Adam shuffled down the stairs at 9 A.M., the other boarders were already out for the day, and Beth and Moira were sitting having tea in the dining room. Beth's face was grim.

"The fire was my fault. Goliath had to have done it. Maybe he brought that cigar inside. The firemen said that the door was open."

"It was. I talked to my wife last night after you left. She said she had come over to talk to me and left it open when she couldn't find me. She didn't know Goliath was there."

"Oh… Wow… What had she wanted to talk to you about?"

"I never asked… so many things. So, I don't know." He stared blankly out through the lace-covered windows onto the lawn.

Beth cleared her throat. "I --we -- have a proposition for you. Moira and I have been discussing it all morning. Since you need someplace to live, and, well, we both have houses.

Um, Moira is not very busy during the week. And you need to be here for work. So, she offered to have you stay with her, free of charge, until you can rebuild. But, on the weekend, she really needs the room and the income and everything. So, if you don't mind driving down to the city every weekend, you're welcome to stay with me. I have an extra bedroom or two." She paused, looking at him expectantly. "Please, let me help. It's the least I can do."

Adam lowered his forehead down onto the floral tablecloth that had replaced the repaired lace one. This extraordinary gesture humbled him. He needed a minute. Tears welled. *She could have just walked away from this whole mess, many times. When he knocked her out, when he was knocked out, when she realized he was married, and now, when he didn't have anything at all to offer except the burden of his presence. But here she was. Offering to put a roof over his head. Arranging a place for him so he could continue to work. Filling the gap for him. Asking for nothing.* He sniffed loudly, and Moira handed him an embroidered cloth handkerchief with green scalloped edges and a swirling vine in the corner. He wiped his nose and looked at them both with grateful, moist eyes.

"I don't know what to say."

"Say you will."

He paused.

"I will."

Beth and Moira both breathed out noisy sighs of relief, then Moira went to the kitchen to busy herself making an egg sandwich and coffee for Adam's late breakfast.

"If you want, my plan is to take you down to Target today so that you will have the essentials, then I'm going to head back to the city to prepare for your arrival. My house isn't exactly, um, ready for company."

"Don't go to any extra trouble on my account! I don't want to cause you any additional work. I'm sure your house is fine. I'm excited to see it."

Beth's stomach lurched. One person's fine, was, well, she just had to get home and start working on it. One week was not going to be enough, but maybe she could clear out the bedroom for him at least, and a clear path to the bathroom.

"And I can take myself to Target, get what I need."

"I really feel like this is all my fault. Please let me start gathering what's been lost."

"It's not your fault. You just got a front-row seat to my implosion."

"I trained my dog to bring in whatever was in the yard, to put it in a box inside. I trained him to do exactly what he did last night. My desire for a beautiful façade made you homeless.

I am responsible, whether you choose to believe it or not. I've decided up here." She pointed to her temple. "And I am determined to do what I can, for my friend. Adam, you brought me out of my self-imposed isolation for the first time in years, and my gain has been your loss. I don't think I can even express—"

"All right. Let's go buy some new clothes, and a toothbrush, just the essentials. But no praise. You're the hero here. You and Moira." He smiled toward the kitchen.

Beth did not accept this title but didn't protest aloud. She had won this battle and didn't want to sabotage it. She was happy to help him start again. Whatever that meant.

The drive was quiet. They were both lost in their own worries. Beth was struggling with how and when to explain about her house. Was there time to hire the people from the T.V. show *Clean Sweep*? Could she watch it all be put into a dumpster in her front yard?

Adam, despite himself, could not stop thinking about the new information he had about Dominique. She was a baby, discarded. Next to a dumpster surrounded by cardboard boxes in a back alley. Sure, she grew up raised by kind, generous people. People that had wanted her, taken her in, treated her with love. But that wouldn't outweigh the symbolism, the knowledge that someone must have valued her on the level of banana peels and expired milk.

They made a turn *up* the hill. Adam looked at her, head tilted to the side in confusion.

"There isn't much cargo room in here. I need to unload what I brought, for the squirrel from the other afternoon. Then we can fill the empty tubs with shopping bags," Beth said.

She pulled up into his driveway next to the Jeep, parked the car, flipped the front seat forward to get the Rubbermaid tubs out of the backseat. She carried one, and he carried the other around the far side of the garage where the caution tape didn't block their way. The only things left were steps leading nowhere. The cement steps up to the front door and the wooden steps down from the missing deck to the grass. They looked like tiny bleachers facing away from the playing field. As if it was too hard, and the spectators didn't want to see what had become of the battling teams. They knelt in the leaves at the foot of the tree that now had charred branches on the house side. They spread the acorns in a slow circle around the base of the tree. It looked a bit like a moat. A tiny sea of nourishment that might be a buffer against the marauders, cold and hunger. Thousands of nuts, gathered and stored for no foreseeable purpose were now serving one. For the first time that she could tell, her gathering would benefit some living creature instead of burying one. It felt like a truly important thing to do, but still she walked back to the car at a fearsome pace, away from the first thing she'd gotten rid of in twenty years. It took every ounce of fortitude she had to not run back and use her arm to sweep them all back into the bins, to throw them back in the car, to drive back to her hibernation, her hermit hole, in order to stop feeling as though a part of her had been extricated and left to rot on the lawn.

This was only the beginning; if she was going to do this, let him move in. There would be countless things she would have to part with. The massive boxes filled with Christmas decorations far too big for *her* house, but that her parents had hung in the vaulted ceilings of their great room. Bin after bin of ball gowns that, while they fit her, she would never wear to any black-tie party. Delicate bone china wrapped in dish towels, settings for more than twenty guests, when she didn't have a clear table on which to place them, or guests to impress, or an accessible stove on which to cook anyone a meal of any kind. Her childhood and loved ones now resided in those boxes, shut up and taped down like her grief. So, with her foot firmly on the accelerator, she and Adam sped away from his house down the patched and misshapen asphalt, Adam mistaking her agitation for excitement, and Beth mistaking his contemplation for indifference.

174

He was thinking about Dom's baby blanket. He assumed it was lost in the fire but hoped it had been saved. It and the basket were the only things she had arrived with, if the article in the drawer was accurate. *Why no explanatory note? Why the dumpster behind an antique store? Why any of it at all?* He wondered how old she had been when Anne had told her where she came from. He worried about that hefty burden being too much for her graceful shoulders. As the country estates whipped past the car window, he wondered what it had been like to grow up in an affluent community where everyone knew her humble and scandalous roots. Here it didn't matter that a person had never done anything wrong, the front porches were still filled with discussion and judgement, and at dinner, people she had never even met had probably prayed for her the confident prayers of the pious and privileged. Pity engulfed him. Somehow this tragic beginning gave her a depth he had never considered, a strength and a courage he had often longed for and lacked in himself.

The Target parking lot was an anthill of families with kids. Beth grabbed a stray cart that a tiny bump or light wind would have sent rolling into a shiny Cadillac. A cart at Target was symbolic; it showed she was serious. There would be no browsing over five-dollar baskets of DVDs strategically placed in the aisle by electronics, no trying on necklaces and scarves, no walking back and forth through the seasonal section that was currently set up for Halloween. As they walked up to the doors, a couple of angsty teenagers were sitting on the giant red cement balls that protect the front doors and watching the cars go by and looking simultaneously bored and angry, vape smoke tumbling from their sneers.

The automatic doors slid open, and they were hit in the face with the smell of buttered popcorn and Starbucks coffee. They were both lovely scents separately but a nauseating combination. Beth hurriedly pushed the cart past the dollar bins and headed to the back of the store and the men's clothing section. Adam followed. She planned to buy him at least one outfit for each day of the week. Just get that first week out of the way for him, let him concentrate on calls to the insurance company, his students, getting to know Moira. They started browsing. She rolled the cart past racks of coats, flannels, swimsuits, workout shirts.

"Fall is a disregarded season," Beth said.

"How so?"

"Well, I mean in terms of apparel at least. There are clearance racks of shorts and t-shirts, and the new bins of sweaters and racks of wool socks. It's like the Thanksgiving of seasons. People start decorating for Christmas right after Halloween anymore. They don't even bother to put anything thankful in the seasonal aisle. They skip right from demanding candy to demanding presents. You know what I mean? Anyway, it seems like everything here is either too warm or too cold to wear right now."

"It will be cold soon enough."

"Truth. But I wanted to get you clothes for *this* week. And frankly, I don't see anything that really works." Beth scrunched her lips to one side, her chin in her hand as her elbow rested on a rack of candy-colored polo shirts.

"Well, let's see... there are these long sleeve cotton dress shirts with the little alligator on them. And some khakis? Really, men's clothes are not that complicated."

"I've often thought that." *Just this side of slovenly.* "I've also often thought maybe I was just born in the wrong era. I mean, look at Cary Grant or Humphrey Bogart. Those men could *dress*."

"You do always seem to be working an ensemble. But, silver lining, a well-dressed person today really stands out."

"Easy to shine, I guess. Have you read *Oliver Twist*?"

"Sure, years ago. Why?"

"Do you remember, in the first chapter, Dickens talks about the power of dress to convey a person's station in life? Wrapped in a blanket, Oliver could have been a prince or a pauper, but as soon as they put him in a dirty workhouse gown, he's 'badged and ticketed' as an inconsequential member of society, worthy to be discarded."

The word 'discarded' was like a sucker punch. It woke him up to his wife's reality. His pity for Dominique was rolling into a cursory understanding. Those clothes. They weren't a spoiled child getting what she wanted. They were a woman on the bottom rung's attempt to raise her own worth. A mask to hide her feelings of inconsequence. They were the stuff of the valued. Why had she kept this from him? He would have gone without food to fill this need, now that he knew it wasn't just a want.

"Are you okay?"

"Just thinking about something. I really could get five of these shirts in different colors and patterns, and a few different pairs of pants." He hung them over the side of the red plastic cart.

"Umm, not to get personal, but don't you need some undergarments? And socks? And are you committed to those Halloween jammies I got you?"

"They're actually really comfortable. Moira's is a bit chillier than I'm used to, and the fleece was nice. So, thank you. Maybe we could look for some fuzzy orange socks to match."

"I like where your head is at." They strolled through the men's department and got the other necessities – there were no orange fuzzy socks, so they got black -- and then headed to get toiletries.

The men's health and personal care aisle was not a place Beth often found herself. She busied herself sniffing all the musky aftershaves and minty shave gels. They reminded her of her dad, like morning coffee and crossword puzzles. Even though he had money, he always bought drugstore staples. Old Spice, Gillette, Sanka. Maybe it was because of the convenience of the Walgreens on the ground floor of their apartment building, or maybe he didn't see the point of spending extra on something no one would ever see.

"Just throw whatever you need in the cart. Is there any other section you need to go to? Do you need snacks? Or lunches for work?"

"No, this should be fine. Thank you so much. Once I get situated and wrap my head around this whole thing, I'll put together a list of stuff I can't manage without. It will probably be short. I'm a bit of a minimalist." But as he walked up to the checkout conveyor belt, Beth was gratified to notice, he threw a bag of Funyuns, a deck of cards, and a Payday candy bar onto the belt behind the separator stick.

As they stood waiting, Beth added a *People* magazine, a book of crossword puzzles, a tiny memo pad that looked like a composition notebook, an eyeglass repair kit, and a pack of rawhide sticks for Goliath. She was a sucker for the random things in the checkout lane. While it must be horrible for parents with small children, it was hilarious to her that they had lip gloss, light-up rubber alligators, matchbox cars, and beef jerky together on display. They should have a sign above them that read, "Impulse Buys Here." She must have 100 round containers of Eos lip balm in a basket in the bathroom she never used, except to store lip balm and a wide variety of soaps and lotions, whole bins of them.

She often wondered what cashiers privately thought about the purchases of their customers. The job couldn't be that interesting, but employee conversations over breaktime snacks might be entertaining. 'Hey, did you see that guy with the Jell-o, garden hose, and water balloons? I bet there's a messy fight in his backyard later.' More than once she had bought 20 extra things to avoid having the two things she needed, fiber gummies and toilet cleaner, let's say, be the only things in the cart. That reminded her of the woman she had seen earlier that fall, with the wine, pork rinds, and pregnancy test. She told Adam about it as they waited and they giggled together at the thought, wrinkling their noses at the thought of that culinary combination enjoyed together. It probably wouldn't be as bad as the buttered popcorn and Starbucks.

The cashier, a teenager wearing a red polo shirt and a bad haircut with hair that clashed loudly with her shirt, interrupted their moment of silliness. "Who are you?" she asked, eyes narrowed.

"Me?" Beth asked.

"Yeah. Hey Mr. Connors."

"Hey," Adam said.

"I'm Beth. Who are you?"

"I'm Claire, and I've known Mr. Connors for a long time. He was my counselor in middle school. But I don't know *you*. I've heard you've been around here for a few weeks, trying to steal him away from his wife—" she continued,

"Just so you know, Mrs. Connors is a wonderful person. She tutored me in math. I wouldn't have passed junior year without her help."

"You've heard? From whom? And we are just friends, not that it's any of your business," Beth protested.

"Just friends? Carrying him off the parade route and buying him underpants? Okay, sure."

"Please do not speculate about things you know nothing about," Beth replied, feeling panicky.

"If I know nothing about it, all I can do is speculate."

"Claire," Adam jumped in, "really, we're just friends. Our circumstances are none of your concern."

"It concerns me that your wife is allegedly living in a ratty hotel, and Jack said he saw you and this lady together on the Ferris wheel."

"We've had a rough couple days. Please just let it be," Adam sighed.

"You're the one who taught me to speak out, express my feelings. Now I'm supposed to shut up because it's inconvenient for you?" Claire asked.

"No, feel free to express away, but we won't be here to hear it. Are you ready, Beth?"

"More than."

And they pushed the cart out through the automatic doors into the evening. The street lights were just starting to turn on, and the intoxicating smells from the Outback Steakhouse across the parking lot came wafting past them. But they were too tired to eat. Plus, it would be just one more place they could be seen together.

Feeling emotionally drained and as though she had done all she could today, Beth was spurred to leave Chesapeake by the thought of the mountains of regret that she would have to move when she got home. She dropped off Adam and picked up Goliath from Moira's, thanked her, apologized to him, again, and took off for the city. After the conversation with Claire, the Target cashier, it felt a bit like running away.

Beth didn't even remember making the drive. She was so tired, and the route was becoming mundane. The sight of her little house, the thought of burrowing inside, away from the world, was comforting. She scooped up Goliath, her bag of Target purchases, her duffel bag, trudged up the walk and stood in the doorway for a minute. The sense of her own inadequacy overwhelmed her. This colossal failure on her part to cope with her life and make boundaries, to live in the present, to be a steward of what she had, was crippling. The bins were barriers to the life she wanted. When she flipped the light switch in her front room, it seemed darker still. The fixture held three bulbs above a glass dome that pointed down, but two were now burnt out and would remain so into the foreseeable future. The weak light it gave could barely penetrate the gloom. She couldn't face it yet. She dropped her bags and went back out to the front screen porch, sitting on the soft cushion of her wicker chair and looking out and away from the pain behind her. *How on earth would she even make a dent in a week? The task was impossibly large. Breathe. How did she attack big projects at work? She needed a list. Which room would she offer him? What could she part with? Where would it go? The squirrel.* She had been mostly okay with surrendering the acorns to their squirrel. Maybe he would like some antiques and childhood toys? *Focus.* She dug through the plastic Target bag, found the memo pad, and started making a list.

Things I can part with   Who I can give them to

½ my childhood toys because: doubles.........Danny

Retired running shoes..Kendra (she can't run in cross trainers)

                                   (Are we the same size?)

Newspapers and magazines.............the library?

Sugar and sweetener packets...........the city women's shelter?

Remaining acorns.......................local squirrels

She would have to call Kendra tomorrow and tell the long story. The one she'd been avoiding. It would be like a trial run for Friday, when Adam walked into her house and would probably turn right around and walk out. After so many years lacking intimacy, cloaked in solitude, her skin had thinned. Rejection would be harder now that she was finally connecting with people. She needed to write. She turned the page on the memo pad and wrote:

Elliptical

by Bethany Morris

Are there no songs for girls on bicycles

For women learning to be strong, to trust other women again

For men trying to forget the past

For the sick who have done nothing wrong

For longing and forgiveness and loss

For boys trying to be men

Because every forward motion pushes back

Every desire to connect - a missed opportunity

All the good deeds met with skepticism

The memories resurface like a shark's fin in dark water

And there is the realization that we are all children

All our progress means nothing

As we slide backward toward mediocrity

Our hearts pound harder all the same.

Heart pounding, she texted Kendra.

Beth: what is your shoe size?

Kendra: 9

Beth: does Danny have tea parties?

Kendra: yes

Beth: perfect. Talk tomorrow on our run? There's a lot to say.

Kendra: ok

No doubt her behavior was once again weird, and once again, her friend seemed to roll with the unconventionality of it. Beth silently thanked her for her grace. Hoped to be able to give her the same one day. She emailed her boss that she needed a personal day tomorrow. She would have to see what she could get done and how much time it would take. Then she sidestepped through the front room, then through the kitchen to the sink. She brushed her teeth, washed her face, and put the memo pad and the Target bag on the boxes on the table. She needed sleep if she was going to get through the emotional tasks of the morning. She picked her way up the stairs and slid through her bedroom door. Goliath followed her and curled up in front of her on top of the duvet, his back to her belly, warming her and calming that anxiety that was rising. She had no idea if this was a possible course of action for her struggling psyche. She was worried about Kendra's reaction. She already missed her tea set, her acorns, and at the same time wished them already gone. As she was setting the alarm on her phone for 5:30, she got another text from Kendra. It was an emoji. A flexed bicep. Beth responded with a winky face before falling asleep.

*   *   *

BEEP, BEEP, BEEP!

She hit the home button and sat up. It was still dark, but she had a lot to do before the sun came up. Goliath just rolled over to where the bed was still warm from her body. She got dressed for running and put her hair in a ponytail. Groggily, she navigated the crowded hallway to the guest room. The door was halfway open, a bin in front of and behind the door. She stepped over the one in the doorway, labeled Mom's china – platinum trim. She loved that set. They were white with a band of platinum around the scalloped edges, simple. They brought class to every gathering. Her mother used to love serving Italian food on them, the bright reds of the tomato sauces, the dark green of the spinach salads just popped off the crisp white background. This was part of the problem. Whenever she went through rooms, boxes, bins, there were the latent but ubiquitous memories that popped up. Without those plates would she remember her mother's pasta and how it looked on these plates? The way the spinning fork made patterns in the sauce, and the parmesan turned pink.

Then her eyes fell on the three bins she needed. They were off to the right stacked on top of one another; all labeled retired running shoes. There must be 50 pairs. Kendra didn't need 50 pairs of shoes, but to do this she was planning to shift some of her burden to others. She would have to hope again for grace.

One by one, she brought them downstairs and stacked them in the screen porch. Then she headed out to the garage. Opening the side door so no one out to get their paper would see inside, Beth found four bins close to the door that were all labeled <u>acorns</u>. She lugged them out into the driveway and set them on the cement while she took the three empty bins out of the back seat and replaced them with three full ones. She stacked the three empty bins next to the garage in the back yard, so they wouldn't be an eyesore and wondered if she'd ever get rid of them, or if she would just fill them with something else. Then she took the fourth full bin and put it on the passenger seat. She suddenly wished she had some huge SUV to aid in her disposal, but the Beetle would work well in the beginning. It would keep her small steps, small. She backed out of the driveway onto the empty street and headed for the city park.

She ran through the park often, and there was a wooded area in the back, close to the gravel parking lot, accessible from a side street. She pulled in and shut off her headlights. Bin by bin, she walked through the woods, dumping acorns as she walked. It seemed like a public service, a gift to the city squirrels and chipmunks. She could give away what others needed maybe. She could free herself a little bit at a time. Four empty bins later, she climbed into the car, triumphant. With all the acorns gone, there was room for seven bins from the house to move into the garage, and she was seven bins closer to a guest room that would accommodate a guest.

Back at home, she opened the front door, and Goliath came running out, patrolling, and then relieving himself. Then he ran back in, because the grass was cold, and curled up on the wicker couch. Beth began loading the three bins of shoes into the car. Goliath watched with interest but didn't get up until she started the car and backed down the driveway again. This was not her routine, and it made him suspicious. She could see his beady eyes reflecting her headlights as she drove toward Kendra's.

She drove slowly through the pre-dawn streets. This was a task she did not relish. It was a risk to expose who she was to someone not obligated to care for her or accept her habits, good or bad. As she parked on the street in the cul-du-sac, between Kendra's driveway and the next, Beth decided to pick out the best pair of shoes and save the onslaught of Nikes and Reeboks for later, after she had told her all of it, if she stuck around. Beth chose a red and yellow pair of Brooks' Launch. They had become her favorite over the last few years, so much so that when the company threatened to discontinue them, she had written them a long email about how they were the perfect shoe for her, how devastated she would be if she couldn't buy pair after pair. This was not like her. She generally didn't complain, never sent her food back, never asked twice for lemon in her water if the server forgot, but shoes were important, they took her places. Well, mainly the same places over and over again. She looked at the shoes on her lap and started to feel anxious that the miles she had gone in this particular pair would be negated if she gave them away. They held her journeys in the sweat of the insole, the scuffs on the rubber soles, the stains on the mesh upper from unavoidable puddles.

It was too much. Maybe the acorns were enough for today. She sat there, car running, in theory ready to enter a new phase in her life, but in reality, far from sure. She was shakily putting the car back into drive when she screamed seeing a face out of the corner of her eye. Kendra jumped a bit into the air, the vertical of a middle-aged woman with no time for herself.

Both women took deep breaths as Beth rolled down the car window.

"You scared me!"

"I gathered. Are you leaving?"

"Yes. No. NO. I came here to tell you things. And to give you things. And to finally open up to someone. Are you prepared for that? Because I can go. I am accustomed to the company of my own mind."

"What are you talking about? Of course, I'm prepared for that. I'm a nurse. I care for people. It's who I am."

Beth looked down at Kendra's sad cross trainers and sighed. Kendra needed these shoes more than she did. Beth didn't need them at all. She had already run 600+ miles in them.

They had served their purpose in her life already. She could share her memories.

"I want you to have these." Beth handed the shoes awkwardly out the window, looking away.

"Thank you! I have never had a pair of shoes just for running before."

"Would you like to try them out with a slow jog?"

"Am I ready for that?"

"Probably not, but we'll take it slow."

Kendra sat on the curb and tried them on, lacing them up tight. She stood up, hopped from one foot to another. "They feel good! Bouncy!"

"Yeah, wearing cross trainers to run is like wearing bricks to swim. Counterproductive. And too heavy. These should help make your first runs a little easier. Ready?"

They started a slow jog out of the cul-du-sac, never even looking back at the cross trainers sitting in the gutter next to the storm drain. They had gone about two city blocks when Kendra's breath started to get raspy, and her face got red.

"Wanna walk?"

"Yeah, for a minute. Thanks for putting up with my newbie lack of skills and endurance."

"No problem. Everyone has to start somewhere. When I started, I ran until I couldn't, probably about as far as we just did, then I stopped and walked to the next driveway, or mailbox, or light post, and started again. I did that for a month or so. By the end of the month, I was running a couple miles without stopping at all. It's a fast progression if you stick with it."

"You make it sound easy," Kendra said, still breathing heavily.

"It's not. But it's worth it. Do I sound like a shoe commercial, or an ad for a CrossFit gym?"

"Shoe commercial." Kendra smiled. "But you're more motivational. Probably because you're not trying to sell me something. Are you?"

"Not sell, but I do have a shoe-related confession that I need to unload. Should we keep walking or sit?" Beth pointed to a park bench.

"Let's keep walking. It probably won't be as intense for you. You'll be able to move through the tension."

"True. Okay, well, here goes. People would probably think it started when I was 20, and my parents died. I inherited all their stuff, two households full. But it started long before that, when they got divorced. It was ugly, bitter. They resented each other so much that they didn't want to see anything from the house of the other. So, they made me have two sets of everything I loved. I traveled back and forth with only the clothes on my back. Years of pondering my habits has led me to the conclusion that that lack of permanence caused even eight-year-old me to want to make *everything* permanent. I started collecting things. Sugar cubes from our tea parties, toilet paper tubes from the bathroom, plastic bracelets from restaurant vestibule vending machines. My parents both kept upscale, meticulously tidy houses, so I couldn't keep things scattered around. For holidays, I asked for makeup cases, tackle boxes, storage bins of all kinds. My walk-in closets became shelf after shelf of containers, containers full of stuff. I didn't need any of it, but I somehow couldn't live without it." She took a deep breath. "I'm a hoarder."

"I think I prefer to call you a woman who hoards. You aren't your weaknesses."

Beth stopped, leaned her elbows against a tall wooden privacy fence, her forehead in her hands, weeping. That simple sentence was exactly the freedom she needed.

Kendra stood close by. Waited for her to work through some of the embarrassment, guilt, relief. Like a restless night leaves a person wrapped in sheets, she needed to untangle.

"I know you have so much to do. But can you help me? I'll help you back, promise. Give you a few nights off to be alone, or just you and Jackson?"

"What do you need?"

"Will you take the bins of shoes in my car? There are three. Pick out whatever you want to keep. Donate or recycle or give away the rest? I have a big job to do. For the first time in 20 years, well, let's face it, ever, I am going to have a house guest. He is staying at my house for the weekends, indefinitely. He doesn't know about my habits, and I need to clear out a room for him. There isn't an empty space anywhere in my house. Three bins lighter would be a huge help. Also, I have a lot of childhood toys, really nice stuff, silver tea sets and china dolls. Would Danny like any new things? I could bring them over when I babysit."

"Whatever you need us to do, really. Danny is a scavenger. She would love nothing better than to dig through boxes of beautiful things. Are you sure that's all I can do? It sounds like a huge project. I have a strong back; I know to lift with my knees."

"You are so sweet. I think I am going to have to work through this mostly on my own. I'm pretty sure the only reason I am even able to let go of these shoes is because you need some. They mean a lot to me. Forrest Gump said they say a lot about a person, right? They tell where they're going and where they've been? I've spent years running in these shoes. Alone. They've carried me away and given me a respite from this life

I have never really fit into, cushioned every footfall. Sorry, I am waxing poetic about old shoes."

"I'll treasure them."

"Thank you."

They started to run again and made it four blocks this time. Kendra was feeling the rush, adrenaline pumping. She started to think, as they paused to walk, about her husband that would never walk again, much less run, and she sped up, running again, faster, filled with the knowledge that not everyone gets to run with their friend on a Monday morning. *But I get to.*

*   *   *

When Adam got to work that morning in his new Target ensemble, he was immediately besieged by hugs from 13-year-olds. They met him in the parking lot, not waiting until he arrived in his office.

"We heard about the fire."

"We're so sorry!"

"Are you okay?"

"Do you know what happened?"

"You can stay at my house. We have a guest room."

"What about your wife?"

Adam tried to shush them and allay their fears. "Thank you, guys. Everyone's okay. It's just stuff. I have a place to stay, and I'll get through this. You are so kind. Get along to class, I don't have this many tardy passes." After they dispersed, he entered the office and saw a giant jar on the counter in front of Jan. Taped on the front was a construction paper sign that read, "Mr. Connors Fire Fund." It looked like there were already more than fifty dollar bills in it. There would probably be lots of kids not buying a cookie at lunch today. He truly admired their sacrifice. Those cookies were not easily passed up.

"Did you do this?" Adam asked Jan.

"The kids. They insisted. They've been waiting for you since the buses started dropping them off this morning. Are you all right?" She got up and hugged him.

"I will be. Just trying to get over the shock. I'm homeless. It's weird to say that out loud. Does anyone need to see me right away or do I have time to make a few calls to the insurance company?"

"Go ahead. Nothing urgent. Let us know if we can help."

He headed down to his office, sat in the chair, looked at the print of *Christina's World* above his desk, decided his life was relatively lucky, and started making calls.

*   *   *

Dominique hadn't wanted to go to her mom's when Adam asked her to leave. She wasn't ready to break her heart. But when the fire happened, she wasn't sure what to do. On one hand, it would be weird for a daughter to stay in a motel after her house burned down since her mom lived in town, but on the other, there would be questions as to why Adam wasn't staying there too. It had to be dealt with. She had to talk to her. At the small accounting firm where she worked, it was hard to avoid her co-workers, but she tried to put off the questioning by saying that everything was okay, that she really had a lot of work to do before her big deadline, that she really didn't feel like talking about it. Late in the day, Stephen called her into his office. She walked glumly past the raised eyebrows of her fellow accountants and into his office. She closed the door softly.

"What do you need?"

Stephen was growing used to her chilly responses and said carefully, "I heard about the fire. I am so sorry. Is there anything that I can do? The firm?"

"No. Thanks. I am handling it."

"I miss you."

"You see me every day."

"It's not the same. You're not really here. Should I be concerned?"

"About what? About me? Or you?"

"About us."

"Yes. There is no *us* right now. I need to get my house in order, figuratively, at least. Can you understand that? I really just can't." She was so tired that she couldn't be compassionate for his broken heart. She was numb.

"I think I do. Please let me know if I can do something, anything."

"Okay. Right now, I need to be left alone."

"Noted."

She turned and walked out of the office, closing the door with a faint click.

After work, she headed to the antique store. She paused outside the back entrance as she almost always did. She stared at the dumpster in the corner, at the cement steps leading up to it and the platform beside it. Sometimes she even climbed the steps and sat on the platform, expecting to see something, but she did not know what.

She slipped through the back door and walked up to the front, careful to avoid the squeaky boards that would alert her mother to her presence, but her mom was not at the desk. She wandered around for a minute, holding the figurines, scanning the books, running her fingers over the old fur coats. The smells here were the smells of her childhood, of nostalgia, but also of decay. Like grocery items that were not yet expired but were far past their *best by* date. She had never understood it, the compulsion to buy old things, but the old houses in this town looked beautiful with the antique glassware behind the wavy leaded glass, and the old farm plows in front yard landscaping conjured a simpler time, so the store did enough business to stay afloat.

Dominique sat down in the rattan-seated rocking chair and started thinking about her future. She had nothing except the clothes that Stephen had bought for her. In the world. Her husband had kicked her out of the house. She was a blank slate. She could head in a new direction and start a new story, or she could try to fix the old and broken tale, giving it new life with an unexpected plot twist. Just then, her mother came up from the cellar with an old barn window. She had a piece of sandpaper and was smoothing the rough edges and chipped red paint.

"Hi, Mom. Whatcha making?"

Anne was interrupted from her focus on the mundane task and looked up. There was watery happiness and pity in her eyes. It was a look that Dominique had learned to value, cherish even. They squeezed each other tightly. Anne pushed her daughter back a bit and put her hands on Dominique's cheeks to get a good look at her.

"I called all over when I heard. I couldn't find you. The fire station told me no one was hurt. Why didn't you call or come by? I was so worried." Anne normally spoke slowly but couldn't stem this flow of words.

"I'm so sorry to make you worry. My cell phone wouldn't charge. The outlets in the motel room are sketchy."

"What motel room? I don't understand. Your room is all ready at our house. Where is Adam?"

"Mom, I need to talk to you. Please, sit down." They sat at an old dining room table in one of the booths, the chairs' cushions were embroidered with roses, and the table was set for eight. "Adam and I aren't doing well. I have been seeing someone else, and he is rightfully angry. Neither of us were home when the fire started because I had been living in a motel, and he was out with a female friend. Now that I think about it, he was probably at the Adele concert that he bought me tickets for, for my gotcha day."

Anne leaned forward, her elbows on the table and her forehead in her hands. Everything she had never wanted for her daughter was now on the table, but she couldn't digest it. Dominique knew what her mother would choose. She would choose to fix what was broken. That old windowpane would probably be repurposed into something beautiful. It could be done if restoration was the goal.

*   *   *

After leaving Kendra and the three bins of shoes, Beth spent the rest of the day trying to clean out the guest room. She removed bin after bin, checking inside to make sure that her labels were correct. She found two bins labeled <u>Toys from Dad's house</u> and brought them down onto the screen porch to bring to Kendra's later, but most of the bins were her dad's things. The garage items were so heavy, whole bins of tools, hammers, screwdrivers, nails. She lugged them down the stairs, trying not to fall, her back leaning against, kind of sliding down really, the banister as she went. It helped to steady her and balance out the weight of the bins. She brought them outside, stacked them in the garage where the acorns had been.

She cleared off the bed and a space about two feet wide all around it. She made many trips with her Beetle, hauling off containers of table and bed linens, towels, curtains. The clothes she left, two towers reaching to the ceiling. Adam was about her father's size and would probably need some nice things as time went on. Maybe in time they could go through the closet, and he could put them in it. For now, though, she couldn't think about it. There was still the kitchen to work on, since she would need to make food and have a place to sit and eat it. When she was done with the guest room, it wasn't perfect. There were still twenty-five bins in addition to the clothes, stacked along the outer walls, full of the more expensive and fragile items. China, crystal, silver, antique clocks, and expensive watches and accessories. There was an entire bin of gold chains, belts with gilded buckles, cufflinks, and money clips.

Beth vacuumed the newly exposed carpet, plugged in a Febreze vanilla air freshener. She opened the windows to let in some fresh air, cold though it was, and removed the curtains and bedding. Back into the Beetle she went, off to the laundromat to finish off today, and say hello to Gwen.

"Gwen, hi!" Beth said, her voice muffled by the pile of curtains and sheets in front of it.

"Hello, dear." Gwen replied, knitting methodically and nodding slowly in her direction. "What's going on? You look like you're dressed to go running."

"Oh, yeah, I never changed from this morning. I'm thinking about taking a little run while the machines are working. This morning wasn't much of a workout. A short run, then a lot of heavy lifting. Not enough cardio for me, though."

"Cardio, shmardio. Want a muffin? My granddaughter made them. Banana nut."

"No thank you. Trying to quit."

"Looks like you never started."

"Thanks, but I am tempted now and then. More by ice cream, though. It's my weakness. When I was little, my dad used to buy me an ice cream cone after every tee-ball game. Blue moon. Now I prefer other flavors, but nothing brings me back like blue moon."

"Well, it seems you only eat sweets once in a blue moon. Ha! Suit yourself. More banana nut for me."

Beth filled two washers with her yards of fabric, inserted her coins, waved to Gwen, and headed out for a night run on a new route.

She felt lighter. The day had been more productive on the clutter front than maybe she had ever had. Maybe there was something to this getting outside herself. She could clearly combat her vices and predilections with another person's happiness as her primary goal. It had been so long since she'd had let anyone close enough to be able to do for them. She tried to reach into her wells of compassion. They were deep and still. It wasn't easy, certainly, but it was possible. She mentally threw coins into the well, wishing for a way out of her life and a continuation of her new friendships and interests. As she pondered this metaphor, she ran in and out of the pools of light under the streetlights, barely noticing the hazards. Her hot breath came out into the night air as fog, visible and moist as she ran through it. Her face was glistening with the condensation, and she wiped her eyes as her lashes started to drip.

She rounded a corner onto a residential street. The houses were well-kept, brick ranches with big backyards. Most had chain-link fences and detached garages, blue television light flickering in the front room picture windows. There were fewer streetlights, but the glow from the houses kept it from seeming too dark and eerie. She stopped to check her pulse and the time in front of a small white house with a little porch and a sconce lit next to the brass house numbers. It was just after nine o'clock, and her pulse was a little fast, so she paused a little longer to take some slow breaths, her eyes closed.

The growling started faintly. She looked around in a panic but couldn't tell where it was coming from. She started to jog forward, away from the sound, but it got louder, and the dog got closer with every footfall. She could feel herself starting to panic; she couldn't see what kind of dog it was, in the darkened street. One thing was for sure, though, it was angry and wanted her away from its property. She felt the animal's paws on her back, felt her shirt pulled violently, like she was the red ribbon in the middle of a tug-of-war rope, struggling to move forward, even an inch.

I cannot be hurt by this animal, she thought. *I live in a home where crutches are not possible. There is so much to do by Friday. There is so much still to do. I cannot let progress slow. I haven't even had time to dream a new dream or make new plans. I cannot lose this battle, or I will lose the war.* She continued to run, twisting her torso to try to shake him free. Her love of things canine was temporarily suspended. She swung her arms, flailing wildly, trying to strike and surprise it enough that it would let go. Beth reached ahead into the darkness, like she was falling and just needed something to grab onto to keep her from the abyss. But there was nothing but cold air and the glow of televisions and the melody of her own struggle.

She felt the fabric of her shirt give way. There was a sickening sound of ripping nylon, like an old rusted zipper, the gentle thud of her knee hitting the grass beside the sidewalk, the soft gasp of fear, the fast and panicked breathing. She imagined her leg being ripped open, bleeding into the grass of an unfamiliar neighborhood, the yard of people she had never met. She would become their lawn litter. *Someone would have to come to her house and clear it out. Even dead, it would be embarrassing.* She pictured the faces of those people, wrinkled noses as they crossed the threshold, appalled at the person who had hidden herself from the world. Would anyone even come? How long would it take before anyone noticed? Would Goliath be okay until Friday when Adam arrived? She wouldn't be able to explain herself. The burden she had created would be someone else's, maybe his. She couldn't. Beth started to crawl forward, hoping to reach the next streetlamp and its welcoming pool of light as the dog, sinking his teeth into the seam under her arm, tried to keep her from it. She hoped she could yell for help and some stranger would hear her. Then a man's voice floated across her fear.

"Chief! Come!" and with a whimper, the dog was gone.

"Miss, are you all right? Can I help you? Miss!" He sounded concerned, sincere.

She wanted to reassure him she was okay. She didn't want him to always wonder if something of his had hurt her. In this moment, free from the very real danger he had just saved her from, she couldn't help him. She couldn't return the favor. She couldn't stay there in that grass and recuperate. She couldn't stop. She couldn't even pause. He stood there on the sidewalk watching, calling after her, even jogging toward her shadow moving away from him, but she kept running and looped back around the neighborhood toward the laundromat. Her compassion for this stranger was superseded by her own flight response, and she marveled that she was still able to run, that her legs were undamaged. She could use her time for forward progress. She was alive. The back of her shirt was gone, but her back itself was only scratched. She threw three coins into her mental well, all quarters. She wasn't wishing new wishes but saying thank you for the wishes just granted. Little wishes every lone runner has wished.

Runners dread that sound, the low growl, fear the unfamiliar dog, fiercely protective and unchained, hope to never meet them when alone, when it's dark. That's why they so often stick to a route or run in parks where dogs must be leashed. So, for Beth, the way back felt like an exoneration. She was still afraid, but it was a fear she had faced and overcome. That experience had shown her something about herself. She would not just curl up and be ripped apart. She was stronger than her fear. And there were fears more fearsome than a dog on a dark street.

Chapter 12

"Everyone thinks of changing the world, but no one thinks of

changing himself."

-Leo Tolstoy "Three Methods of Reform"

While Beth waited for Adam to arrive on her doorstep that Friday evening, every fear was bubbling on the surface of her skin. As she sat on the screen porch, Goliath on her lap, bouncing her leg so he couldn't lie still, she was sweaty and itchy and cold. The week had been full of moving, rearranging, and figuring out how to part with some of the stuff she had spent decades accumulating. She was by no means done; the full days at work left her only evenings to make slow progress, and the fatigue that comes with anxiety had left her without a spring in her step. Of course, it may also have been the sorrow of the process. There was no professional organizer to remind her of why this task was necessary, no threat of eviction or job loss, or no worry about foster care for the children she had never felt worthy to bring into the world. Every step was an act of sheer will. Every time she walked down the stairs with a bin, a part of her felt the loss. Like a child, when the tooth fairy leaves them a dollar but they would really love to keep that chunk of bone and enamel for themselves, because it's a piece of them.

She had managed to clear the stairs and the bathroom next to Adam's room. There was a shallow path next to one bank of kitchen counters so that she could access dishes, sink, and stove. Her bed was again piled high, so the couch was once again her bed, but there was always next week, and the next. She was determined to keep pulling forward, even as her past tried to pull her back. She had practiced her explanation, but it was only in her head. Too late, she thought she should have tried it out on Kendra first. A trial run would have made this encounter easier. Or maybe not. It was a moot point anyway. He would be here any minute. She sipped her tea and tried to focus on *Anna Karenina*, but Anna's crises seemed too distant to distract her. She shifted her weight on the wicker couch cushions and could hear the shifting of each piece of willow branch, carefully woven.

"Why is wicker so pretty, but so uncomfortable? Adam will be here soon. Be on your best behavior. Do you want to do one last look around the yard? First impressions, you know."

Goliath wagged.

"All right, out you go."

He started his patrol on the steps, scanning the grass for debris. Nothing caught his eye. Then he started pacing back and forth across the lawn, nose to the ground. There was no peppermint schnapps bottle today, but he smelled the same smells in that same area. He made smaller circles, snout deep in the grass. There was something down under the blades of grass, it was shiny, round. He hooked it on his bottom teeth, brought it up and onto the screen porch. A thick band of yellow gold, scratched and worn through many years, smelled of peppermint, and Tony, and despair.

Tony from around the corner had been suffering through those past weeks. He was exhausted from trying to pretend that nothing was wrong as he sat around the dinner table and ate food they couldn't afford, then watched cable t.v. - a luxury he couldn't give up. His daughter loved the Disney Channel, watched Phineas and Ferb every day. When Phineas told Ferb that he knew just what the day would bring, Tony was in agreement. He just wasn't happy about it. The endless want ads for jobs that he wasn't qualified for tormented him. The long lines at the unemployment office, full of people fresh out of luck and short on hope. Finally, he couldn't take it anymore. Last night he sat down with his wife. He explained his pain, detailed his struggle. To say that she was unsympathetic would be a massive understatement. She was angry that he had lied, scared about the debt that had been racked up in the interim, worried about their house, their daughter's future. She blamed him. He already blamed himself. He needed compassion. She had none to give. When she walked out the door, taking their daughter by the hand, headed to her mother's house, something cracked inside him. The peppermint schnapps couldn't repair it. The family's security had been balanced insecurely over a precipice. They had lived as if tomorrow would take care of itself. Now he wished he'd taken more control. In his anger and defeat, he flicked his wedding band into Beth's yard, hiding the end of his marriage like he did his drinking, hoping to preserve a facade that no one was even looking at.

Beth was shaken from her reverie when she heard something clink into the bottom of the box of front lawn litter. Curious, she dug through the little bottles and found the ring at the bottom, fallen inside the little patent leather shoe. She picked it up, slid it onto her thumb, spun it around. It was about five sizes too big, even for her thumb, but she loved the weight of it, the smooth edges. She turned the light on, looked for an inscription. As the porch light reflected off the shiny interior of the band, she strained to see any letters, any clue as to the owner. There was none. But she was still searching when gray eyes peered through the screen door, searching for her. She was taken aback by his gaze, as he was to see her with a wedding band in her fingers. His face revealed his shock, and she stumbled over her words in explanation.

"Hi, uh, Adam. Welcome to my home. Goliath..umm..found this in the yard. He brought it inside to me."

"Oh, okay," he said, relieved.

"I meant it about the friends thing. Really," Beth said. He laughed and pulled open the door, patting Goliath on the head as he sat on the couch next to her. "So how was your week with Moira?"

"We got to know each other a little. I was working a lot, catching up on sleep, making calls to the insurance company. It wasn't a great time to get to know me. I was quite wrapped up in my own stuff. Next week should be better. The shock is wearing off."

"What did the insurance company say? Are you going to be okay to rebuild the house, replace your beautiful things?"

"There was no sign of foul play that the firefighters and investigators could find, so they will pay out the insured amount, enough to replace everything. The main sticking point will be, of course, what we decide to do, Dominique and me. We are kind of in limbo right now and have nowhere really to meet and work things out. I think she has moved back in with her mother, so talking there will be crazy awkward. This is really a discussion we should be able to have around our dining room table, not the ashes of it."

"That sounds so hard. I'm really sorry." She truly did feel bad about everything, but in the back of her brain, and right behind her in the house, was her real trauma. The information she was terrified to share.

"I don't blame you. Or Goliath, or Dominique, really. I truly believe that things happen for a reason, and there must be some reason for this. It is my catalyst for change. It will force us to deal with the deeper issues as we rebuild our lives, literally from the ground up. We--"

"I have a confession." Beth interrupted. She couldn't delay it any longer. "My house, it isn't beautiful like yours was."

"It doesn't matter to me. I'm just so thankful for a place to sleep. You have no idea how grateful I am. What I've seen so far, your yard and porch, are lovely. I'm sure you will be a gracious host."

"You don't understand. It's a smokescreen, all of it. Everything I show the world. You are actually the first person I've ever let inside my house. It's that bad."

He laughed nervously. "I don't understand. What's bad?"

"Maybe it will be easier to show you." Beth pushed open the door with a heavy sigh, letting him enter before her.

Adam picked up his reusable Target bag that passed for luggage and followed her inside. It took a minute for his eyes to adjust to the dim light. At first it seemed like no lights were on, but when he flicked the switch, it got darker. He flicked it back. Beth hadn't touched the front room. The air was close and acrid. The bins seemed to be leaning toward him, looming over him. He squinted to read the labels in the first tower of bins, dog leashes and bowls, miscellaneous paper products, phone books. *Phone books? Who in the hell even used a phone book anymore?*

"It started in here," she said, "I rarely used this front room, so I would store what I wasn't using but couldn't part with in here. Before my parents passed, it was just little things. I couldn't throw away the old phone book, because what if I needed an address or a number that wasn't in the next edition? What if a business closed, and I couldn't remember its name?"

"Okay, well, what about Siri?"

"I'm not a technophobe, really, I just needed to keep them. Like books you've already read and may never read again, but can't part with, you know?"

"Did you read the phone book?"

"No, but -- it's hard to explain." It was silent for a long time as they stood there in the near-dark.

"Look, Beth, I'd be lying if I said this is what I expected to find, but in my college courses I learned quite a bit about compulsions, and maybe I can try to help you while you help me."

"You're not leaving?" Her eyes widened.

"No. I think I can help, and honestly, I have nowhere else to go." He paused. "Can you show me the rest of the house?"

"Sure. Most of it. I have been trying all week to clean out a space for you. I hope it's okay." Her breathing slowed as her worst fears were not realized. She had expected to watch his taillights recede into the distance. *He was still here. He may even help.* She was not abandoned, not alone anymore.

She led him through the front room and into the sunken family room. Adam's eyes followed the narrow path to her couch, her sheet and blanket pitifully tucked into the cushions, and on the floor below it, Goliath on his unicorn bed. The little dog looked up then, disinterested, curled back up and returned to sleep.

"Do you cook much?" he asked as she led him into the kitchen, accessible but stacked high with boxes of kitchen things, there was a box labeled spatulas, and what seemed to be many filled with individual free packets, <u>sugar</u>, <u>ketchup</u>, <u>jelly</u>, <u>honey</u>.

Brutal honesty. "No, I eat mostly take-out or bag salad. Would you like some tea though? I have lots of different flavors."

"That sounds good, but maybe later. Is there a bathroom on this floor?"

She fought the urge to make the tea anyway. Those sweeteners may finally start to dwindle now. It was too exciting. "Yes, right here." She opened the first door in the hall. It, too, was full to the top with boxes, but the sink was empty, and the toilet could be used if the user's legs weren't too long.

As they rounded the corner, the stairs seemed like a wide-open promenade. They were completely free of any bins, freshly vacuumed, and the banister gleamed. At the top of the stairs, she gestured toward the closed door.

"This is my bedroom. It is too full to use right now, so I sleep downstairs. Your room is here." She pointed to the room across and down the hall. The door was open wide, and the bed was freshly made. The bins against the walls were still there, but there was plenty of room to move around. "These bins are full of my dad's clothes." She pointed to the three bins stacked by the closet. "If you need something nicer than what we bought last week, please use whatever you can. My dad cared a lot about how he presented himself, so everything looks pretty timeless, even though it's older."

"Thank you."

"There's a bathroom across the hall, I cleaned it out too. And I plugged a small nightlight in the hallway, so you can navigate. There's still so much to walk around. I tried, but one week wasn't enough to make much of a dent."

"I appreciate it."

"Well, that's really all there is to see. Do you think it will be okay just for the weekend? I'll do more next week. Do you still want that tea?"

"Let's call it a night. I'll have some in the morning."

"Okay. Thanks, Adam. For staying."

"Thanks for having me. I know this probably hasn't been a cakewalk for you either."

She nodded and left him to get ready for bed, heading down her open stairway with no fear of falling.

Chapter 13

"The whole world is a series of miracles, but we're so used to them
we call them ordinary things."

--Hans Christian Anderson

"Chesapeake Middle School, Mrs. Talbot speaking -
What can I do for you?"

"Jan, this is Dominique... Connors."

"Oh, hi! Are you okay? Adam left for the day already,
since it's Friday, you know. Were you looking for him?"

"I'm fine, thanks. I actually had a question for you.
And I was wondering if we could keep it on the down-low."

"Of course! I'm a locked vault of information. What's
up?"

"Could you by any chance tell me where Adam is
staying? Please don't ask why I don't know."

"Well, should I unlock the vault?"

"I'm his wife, Jan."

"Of course. He's staying at the Bed and Breakfast on
Catalpa Street. The cute Victorian."

"Hmm, okay, he told me that, but I called there, and the
woman said he is not currently staying there. Weird."

"You should just go over there and question her. That's where he told us he'd be."

"Do you think this has anything to do with that runner he's been hanging around with? I've heard lots of rumors. Do you know anything?"

"All I know is she's apparently really strong, you know, fit, according to parade-goers anyway. A few weeks ago, she supposedly saved Therese's kid at the apple orchard. The younger one, I think. Um… Oh! She likes to go to Beantown. That's all I've heard, promise. The lady at the B&B is named Moira. Gotta go, someone on the other line. Bye."

Dom had been driving during the whole conversation, and by the time Jan hung up, she was sitting in her car in front of Moira's B&B. She jangled her keys nervously as she strode up the front walk, then used her knuckles on the door instead of the knocker. Three loud raps. No one answered. She turned the knob. Poked her head in. "Is anyone here?" she shouted to the empty foyer. She heard music playing in another part of the house. *I can go in, right? This is a place of business. Or is it a private home? Am I trespassing?* She walked in, tentatively. She walked through the dining room toward the music. It was loudest at the entrance to the sunroom. A woman's back was to her. She desperately didn't want to startle a woman whose hair was so gray, but she'd come too far to turn back. She knocked on the glass of the French doors.

The older woman wheeled around. When Moira's eyes fell on Dominique, she squeaked and fell back into the patio chair. She threw her hands up over her face as though she could hide.

"I cannot," she whispered, turning away.

"I'm so sorry to startle you," Dominique said. "I won't hurt you." The reaction had been more than just that of a woman who thought she was alone in the house. Moira was visibly uncomfortable, and Dominique's forehead furrowed in confusion. "I knocked, but no one answered. I'm looking for my husband, Adam Connors? Are you okay?" She looked down at the shaking woman in her flowered house dress and wished she hadn't come. "Can I help you?"

"I – I've never seen you so close up," Moira stammered.

"What do you mean? Do I look hideous or something?"

"No, my goodness, you're the most beautiful young woman I've ever seen. Your taste is impeccable. That dress, it's perfect. You grew up just right."

"You're making me a little uncomfortable. I appreciate the compliments, but I don't think I've ever seen you before," Dominique admitted.

"I am sorry. Can I make you a cup of tea? Let's get to know each other since your husband will be staying with me for a while. Would you like to stay too? Or are you already comfortable somewhere else? I have extra rooms during the week. I'm so sorry about the fire."

"Um, well, I don't drink tea, but thank you, maybe just water?"

Moira scuttled over to the record player and lifted the long arm off the Jackson Browne album she'd been listening to. The sound of ice cubes clinking into a glass tumbler rang from the kitchen. Dominique wandered in. "About Adam, is he here?"

Moira set the water glass down on the counter next to her. She was starting to gather her composure. "Not right now, he's staying in the city for the weekend with a friend. I am booked up on weekends as we head into the holidays, so I told him he could stay here during the week."

"Can I ask how you know him?"

"It's a small town."

"But you don't know me."

Moira quickly changed the subject. "Have you met her, Adam's friend? Beth?"

"No. I haven't. Is she a friend of yours too?"

"She is. A new friend. Truly a good person. Very athletic. Has a little dog. He's so sweet. She keeps him in her handbag like a toy. Normally I don't encourage pets, but he just couldn't be better behaved."

Dominique tried not to think about the dog bed on her flawless wood floors, the open door, the flames, the regret. *She couldn't play the jealous wife. She had given up that right when she had taken up with Stephen, and yet, she was jealous. They were together right now, maybe training for a damn half-marathon or something. She couldn't have it both ways. Either they had exclusive rights to each other, or they didn't. There were no halfsies. Marriage was a two-way street or some other stupid cliché. She decided. She wanted it back. Hackneyed truisms and all.* "So, he'll be back on Monday? Will she be here as well?"

"Yes, and no. She works in the city. Just Adam will be back, Sunday night after my guests leave. Pretty sure he has to work on Monday. Still a few weeks until vacation, right?"

"Yeah." *There would be no twinkle lights from the little balcony this year. No stockings, no luminaria along the front walk, no faculty Christmas party, no presents. Not for her anyway.* "Thanks for the information and the water. I'll let you know if I need a room. I'm so sorry I startled you. I'll let myself out." She sped to the front door, needing to get out into the cold air and clear her head. The interaction was so unsettling, so creepy, she practically ran to her car.

Moira watched her go, relieved to be alone and terrified that Dominique wouldn't come back.

*   *   *

Beth carried two steaming cups of tea out onto the frigid screen porch Saturday morning.

"It's getting too cold to sit out here." A shiver ran up Beth's back, almost spilling their tea.

"It's not too bad. I think we can handle it. You look ready to run." Beth had her winter running gear on; her ponytail bobbed through the hole in her running beanie as she nodded.

"I hate to leave you alone, but I'm sort of a creature of habit."

"So I gather. Go ahead. I brought *The Count of Monte Cristo* to keep me company."

"Well, if I'd known you kept such fancy company, I would have brought out the Earl Grey." Beth set out on her run, earbuds in to keep her feet on pace and to keep the wind out of her ears.

On the porch, Adam shivered and sipped his quickly cooling tea, wondering if there was a bin of afghans somewhere. He saw two tubs on the floor of the porch, past the door. The labels weren't visible, so he went over and opened one. He felt like a child opening presents Christmas morning. Every toy a little girl could want. The silver tea set is what caught his eye first. He flipped it over. FAO was stamped on the bottom. There was a rolled-up rug piano, a Cabbage Patch doll in perfect condition even though it had been removed from its packaging, bags of Legos, a Sony Walkman, a huge canister of pop beads. For an eighties kid, it might as well have been Monte Cristo's treasure. Some of it was probably pretty valuable now, too. He wondered what she was going to do with it. If she was just going to donate it, maybe she'd let him sell it on eBay and make some extra cash. *Would a hoarder donate things? Was she in recovery? Had he played some part in her motivation to change?* The other bin had remote control cars, a ukulele, vintage Barbies with more outfits than he currently owned, most with bold Pucci-inspired patterns and go-go boots, and a Barbie horse with a real leather saddle. This was some pretty cool stuff, really. If she was going to hoard, this was much more interesting than phone books and ketchup. He resolved to talk with her this weekend or next, if she seemed open to an impromptu therapy session. Maybe he could figure out the root of the problem, what her triggers were, and help to ease her struggle. She was such a wonderful person, rescuing him at the parade, letting him stay here, saving stranger's children; it seemed a shame that she had been isolated for so long. Marooned on an island of memories, cool Barbie horses notwithstanding.

He wandered inside, made his way to the kitchen to warm his tea with the remaining kettle water, and slowly climbed the steps to his room. Beth probably wouldn't mind him going through the bins in his room. After all, she left them there and trusted him with them, with her whole house really. The porch bins had piqued his interest, and he had the nagging feeling that he would be doing her a favor to get rid of some things. *Seriously, how long had it been since she had looked in those bins in the front room, decades? All those in the back could be empty for all she knew. The ones in his room were her father's; all the labels said so. She carried herself like she came from money. Certainly not every kid has a sterling silver tea set from FAO Swartz for stuffed animal tea parties. Dominique would have loved a childhood like that. Surrounded by beautiful things. Always knowing she was loved and wanted. Not feeling like trash, but rather cherished.* In the doorway of his room, he scanned the twenty-plus bins for the most promising labels. He pulled two out of the stack by the window. One was labeled <u>Accessories</u>, the other <u>Collectibles</u>. He lifted the lid of the former. Jackpot. Just on the top were cuff links, gold money clips, silk ties, rings, gold chains, and polished wing tips. In the corner, though, the pièce de resistance, a beautifully crafted platinum watch with a glass face that showed the sparkling precision mechanisms underneath. *Was Beth's dad the guy in the Dos Equis commercials?* Every item made him more curious.

He didn't know what to expect in the second bin. Maybe he also had collections of Splenda packets like his daughter, but somehow Adam doubted it. He was right to be doubtful. His grin was wide as he peeked under the lid. Inside was a finely crafted humidor full of Cuban cigars. Underneath it was a case containing a huge collection of vintage Zippo lighters. Another under that had pocketknives, Swiss Army knives, and Leatherman tools. Beth was storing a fortune in plastic tubs. Just a box or two of this stuff would buy Dominique the best shoes on Rodeo Drive. And a trip to walk down it. She deserved a red carpet, to be treated like a celebrity, more than he had given her. He was carefully placing everything back just as he had found it when he heard the screen door slam. Then he heard the kitchen faucet, then footsteps on the stairs. He lay down on the bed with his book, head propped up on the pillows. She poked in her head.

"How was your run?"

"Chilly, but interesting. I think my eyelashes froze shut at one point. The winter is coming on fast. I don't know why it surprises me, but it always does.

"I remember back when I was a kid, though, and we had to wear our snowsuits underneath our Halloween costumes. Do you remember that? My mom always made my costume two sizes too big to accommodate it."

"I guess we're lucky it waited this long. I am just dreading scraping the car and shoveling. People die doing that, you know."

"You have a garage, right? Could you put your car in there? Or is it full like most people's?"

"It's full. But I wouldn't say it's like most people's. It looks like my front room, but the bins are full of garage stuff, so they're really heavy. Confession: that's where I got the acorns for your squirrel. And to make room this week, I brought out several other bins of acorns and dumped them in the park so that I could move some of the house bins out there." She looked at her feet, wondering what he thought of her.

There was a long pause that frightened her.

"How brave you are," he said softly. "What do you think allowed you to do that? I assume you'd held onto them for a long time."

"I don't know really. I guess a combination of things. You coming, the squirrel needing them, plus I've been just feeling happier and lighter since I met you and my friend Kendra. I actually gave her a few bins of my old running shoes, and I have a couple bins of toys for her daughter on the porch. I think the only reason I can part with those is because I have two sets of everything. There are duplicates in my bedroom, I think. From my mom's house."

"Divorce?"

"Yeah."

The onion of his new friend was starting to peel back some layers. Before long it was going to make someone cry. Maybe he really could help. "So, it sounds like you are seriously generous. I mean, you seem to be able to let go of some things for others. That's altruistic. If I were in your shoes, I'd be really proud. You're making huge strides."

"It doesn't so much feel like it. I feel like every step forward is another step back. I'm mostly just moving stuff around. Like a little kid at the dinner table, pushing food around her plate. It looks like progress, but maybe the peas are just hidden under the mashed potatoes."

"You don't give yourself enough credit. You are remarkable." He looked straight into her eyes, "I'm so glad we're friends."

228

She looked away. "I really thought once you came inside, you'd turn right around and walk out. I've had a fear of abandonment my whole life, and because of that, I've isolated myself. You have really helped me to see that while my living situation isn't perfect, that I may be salvageable. That my worst fears are not necessarily always going to become my reality. Thank you for that."

"I don't know that I did much, but – you wanna try something?"

"Sure. But you don't give yourself enough credit. **You** are remarkable." She grinned.

"Using my own words against me? That's my job." He grinned.

"What are we trying?"

"What if you just took one bin a day? If the goal for the day, after work and everything, was just to find someone who needed that one bin. You could start in the family room. Then you'd open up a space to entertain your new squad. Hashtag squad goals, amirite? That's what my students say. I know it sounds silly coming from a middle-aged man, but they are just so charming, you know? It rubs off, their little isms."

"I believe you. I haven't spent much time with kids, even when I was one. But Kendra has a little girl named Danny, and she is so full of dreams and happiness. I aspire to be like her, actually. She may have started this whole movement toward wellness. The bucket I got her may be the first thing I'd been able to part with in years. The thought of her happy and playing with those toys in the midst of her difficult situation just makes me feel so, I don't know, useful."

"You wanna try then? It'll be like a game. You don't have to be in a hurry. Just slow and steady progress. Evaluate all you have. Try to decide what brings you joy. Decide what good you can do with it. Maybe you can make it all a big philanthropic gesture. When I'm in Chesapeake, you can update me, and I'll provide support and encouragement."

"Okay. I'm in. I think I should start today, get some momentum. I have some ketchup packets or sweetener packets that I could donate to a local shelter or food pantry or something. I had put that on my list of things to try to get rid of but hadn't gotten around to it. You don't use Splenda, do you?"

"No. Just cane sugar for me."

Without even changing out of her running gear, they immediately loaded the car with two bins from the kitchen, enough Splenda and ketchup for ages, and headed South toward the city.

As they headed down I-75, classic rock station on the radio, they were singing along like an episode of Carpool Karaoke, Eric Clapton's "Layla" on full blast. They smiled at each other, swayed back and forth, feeling good about the task before them and each other.

"Might want to slow down," Adam said. There were brake lights ahead and lots of orange signs and barrels. A big DETOUR sign and an arrow pointed west. Beth didn't feel very knowledgeable about the layout of the city when she got off the highways and her regular routes and was hesitant to make the turn, but there was no choice. Everyone was funneled onto a road she did not recognize.

"We won't get lost. Just follow the crowd," Adam reassured her. He was even less familiar with the area, but really didn't want to put a damper on their wonderful day and her forward progress. However, his positive attitude didn't stop every street they turned on from having less signage, less traffic, making the route less clear. Eventually they lost it altogether.

"My car doesn't have a GPS, and my phone is dead. I truly don't know which way to go," Beth admitted.

"We left in such a hurry, I didn't even bring mine."

"Well, let's just keep driving until something looks familiar. I've been down here enough. The city is just so *huge!*"

After five or six more turns, they ended up on a wide street with a parkway in the middle and buildings on either side with burn marks above the boarded-up windows. There were no landmarks or street names she recognized. Stopped at a red light, Beth shrugged her shoulders and wondered if there were working phone booths anywhere anymore. The last time she needed one was a situation sort of like this, lost with a dead phone battery. She found a gas station with a phone booth, only to realize there was just a severed cord inside. She went inside the station and asked what to do. The young clerk allowed her to use his cell. Everything was fine.

Just then she jumped in her seat as a very tall man pounded on her window. She rolled down her window,

"Hi, can I help you?" Beth asked.

"Hello, um, this is a cute car and everything, but you need to get out of this neighborhood. Now."

"Okay," she said, stunned and suddenly a little shaken, "but I don't know how." She looked up at him pleadingly as Adam sat there, mute and wide-eyed.

"Got a paper or napkin or something and a pen?"

Adam handed one over to him. He sketched out a quick map.

"Sir," Beth said, "I really appreciate your help. I'll turn around up here in this parking lot."

"No. Right here. In the median."

"Okay. Bless you." Beth handed the napkin to Adam and whipped the Beetle around in the frozen grass. She had always felt safe in the city, and this experience strangely made her feel more so. She chuckled a bit as they found their way back to the highway. Her car wasn't exactly one that allowed her to blend in. She hadn't even thought about how it might look to people as she drove by, her giant hydrangea visible through the windshield, maybe silly and self-indulgent. But she was neither. Well, not silly, anyway.

"Do you want to head home?" Adam asked as they reached the north and south on-ramps.

"No, I'm good," she said. *And so are people.* And turned south.

*   *   *

As they pulled onto the cracked pavement of the soup kitchen parking lot, Beth sighed. The building was an old factory that had made car parts. The windows lined the lot-facing wall, square and cloudy. A couple were broken and covered with the thick cardboard of an apple box. People deserved more than this.

They entered the massive room lined with long tables and metal folding chairs. The bright light shining through the wall of windows made it feel cheerier, despite the fact that inside it was still uncomfortably chilly. The woman in charge, it seemed, walked over to them with a purposeful stride. She was wearing a hair net and an apron over her street clothes.

"Welcome to Heaven's Kitchen. I'm Kim. Can I help you? You hungry?" Beth and Adam could see the steaming dented chafing dishes filled with mixed vegetables and baked noodles and cheese. At the end of the counter was a little sign. *Desserts donated by Skyline Bakery.* There were cupcakes, cookies, and pastries, all arranged on tiny plates.

"We don't need anything, thanks," Beth replied. "I actually called you yesterday. I have a bit of a collection of condiments and sweeteners, you know, free restaurant packets? I am not using them myself, so I was hoping that you could use them. I see you have a coffee pot over there. I have LOTS of Splenda."

"Oh, yes! I didn't talk to you, but Janelle did and relayed the message. Of course, we could use them. Do you need help bringing them in?"

"No, thank you. We can handle it. Where should we put them?" Kim pointed to a metal shelving unit in the adjoining room.

Out by the car, Adam grabbed the sweetener bin. "Should we stay and help serve dinner?"

"We definitely should. 'One good turn' and all."

They got settled behind the tables, with their own hair nets and aprons. Adam served the noodles, while Beth oversaw the desserts. A family came in mid-meal in a long line. They were bundled up against the cold. Beth counted, *8...9... Nine kids! What a colossal undertaking.*

"Hello, Ma'am, can I get you a treat for after dinner?" Beth asked.

"Nah, thank you. Rather save that sweet mess for the kids," the mother replied.

Beth wondered how often the kids really got to celebrate with sweet treats. She set aside the cupcake with the most sprinkles for the littlest girl -- the one at the end of the line with the braids. She reminded her of Danny. Her big smile revealed missing front teeth, but it didn't stop her from exuding joy. In the line, she twirled. *Twirling may be the most underrated of movements.* Her eyes widened as Beth put the overly sprinkled cupcake on her plate. It was yet another small thing Beth was delighted to give away.

She realized then that the bins holding her condiment and sweetener donation were still in the other room. She hadn't asked for them back, hadn't even thought about them. She hadn't worried about bringing them home and shuffling other stuff into them or refilling them. She had just, without a thought, let them go.

On the way to the car, she twirled across the asphalt. On the way home, no empty bins in the back seat, Beth began to allow herself to hope.

"Maybe I can do this," she said, more to herself than to Adam.

"Looks to me like you already are."

Chapter 14

Ditch the routine. It's the uncertainty we need to keep us excited

about each new day.

On Sunday morning, Adam emerged from the guest room with dark circles under his eyes and carefully shuffled down the stairs holding tightly to the railing.

"I'm exhausted."

"Sorry to hear that," Beth replied, looking up from the paper she had just started getting delivered so he could read it. She was happily ensconced in a fluffy robe and slippers, so she handed over the paper and pulled them tighter around her on the cold morning. Weak light filtered through the frosted glass and lace curtains of the kitchen window. "Want to talk about it?"

"No biggie, just my brain wouldn't shut off last night. I have a lot to think about, and it seems that the middle of the night is when my mind wants to manage it all."

"Been there. Well, I have a run then an afternoon planned with Kendra, Jackson, and Danny, so if you want to spend the day in bed, there will be no judgement here. I'm actually about to head out. Unless you need me to stay and keep you company?"

"No, no. I'm good. Have fun with your friends. I need a chill day anyway."

"Do you mind letting Goliath out now and then?"

"Of course not, we're getting to be buddies." Goliath eyed him suspiciously. Adam shrugged. Beth smiled and turned to head out on her run. The screen door slammed behind her as she left.

"What should I do today, buddy?" he asked while simultaneously judging himself for talking to a dog that wasn't even his. Goliath proceeded to lick his own feet as if they weren't perfectly clean, ignoring Adam and making him feel even sillier.

The thoughts he'd had the night before were hatching a plan in his now fully awake mind. All he could think of was Dominique, the life she had lived and the secrets she had kept. He wanted to change it, to show her her true worth. She seemed to derive value and purpose from beautiful, expensive things. He needed to be the one to provide them. He needed to detach her from the rich man he was sure she didn't really love. Or at least she didn't love that guy like she loved **him** once upon a time. He couldn't spend the insurance money on things that wouldn't last though. He was lovesick, but not impractical. What other money did he have? His salary kept them comfortable, not flush. Right now, he was literally homeless and had seven outfits to his name. Designer clothes didn't make sense. But he couldn't let her go on believing that her value was an equation computed with a dumpster as the constant. She had to know what a jewel he thought she was.

Thinking of jewelry always brought him back to the night he proposed. He was all in. So ready to be bound together forever. If it was possible, he'd possessed even less back then. He jumped in that night despite a mountain of student debt and a job that filled his emotional bucket but not his bank account.

They'd met months earlier at a faculty pool party. She was friends with the host, his colleague, Heather, who taught math in the STEM wing. Poolside, she had one of those restaurant margarita machines that magically never seems to run out. In reality, Heather was just very good about keeping it topped off with tequila. After a couple drinks, he saw

Dominique from across the yard. She was wearing a silk wrap over her swimsuit, and she moved from poolside chaise to refilling the charcuterie board with equal grace. It was all over for him then; he was sure of it.

That winter, in the middle of the most Hallmark snowstorm, with big fat flakes and no wind to keep them from falling, spinning, and sparkling, Dominique and Adam walked through Chesapeake, letting the snowflakes land on their faces. They had just seen the movie *Titanic*, and she was crying a little. It was a pretty cry, calm with just a slight chin wobble and a couple fat, slow tears. She had desperately wanted them both to survive and stay together. She had wanted an ending that didn't make sense. She had wanted the fairy tale.

When Adam knelt in the snow on the city park gazebo steps, she got it. She got her own happy ending. She forgot that Jack had sunk to the bottom of the Atlantic. She forgot that Rose had to go on without him. She was rescued from her own sinking ship. She was loved. She yelled, "Yes!" She meant it.

However, while the ring was a symbol of that love, the yellow gold and the chip of diamond that he could afford at the time had lately become a source of regret for him. He wished he'd been able to show her, with a platinum band and a big, *ostentatious rock, that she was valuable beyond measure, that she was worth the debt he never wanted to incur, that she was more than his measly two months' salary. That he would never throw her away. He couldn't. Not even now.*

But now, now he needed to show her. He needed to win back her heart, one that didn't believe it deserved his love, and he had decided that he knew how to do it. He headed upstairs. In his guest room, he started with the bins of Beth's father's things. He chose the most expensive items, things he hoped wouldn't be too sentimental. He was helping her, really. She wanted to get out from under it all. What was she going to do with a man's watch or a humidor? Honestly, would she even remember what was in those bins? Would she miss it? He decided she wouldn't. He decided he could solve both of their problems with one fell swoop.

Adam got out his phone, took pictures, and started listing the items he chose on eBay and Facebook Marketplace. There was at least $100,000 worth of high-end GQ menswear in this room. He reasoned that if she could only get rid of things when other people needed them, well, he needed them. And they were friends. They could enjoy a concert together, spend hours hiking through the orchard, keep each other's secrets. She would want to help him. He was sure of it.

He heard the door close downstairs, the shower, some shifting of bins in her room, the door again, and she was off to Kendra's, and he was back to work.

*　　*　　*

Those first couple of weekends, he made more money than he earned all year working at the school. During the week, he made daily trips to the post office, mailing her memories from Los Angeles to Dubai. He became a Top Seller with five stars on his eBay seller's page and amassed hundreds of satisfied and delighted reviews. It was too easy. Beth never invaded his privacy and entered his room. She never asked what he was doing when he decided to spend the afternoon alone up there. She was used to being alone, and she knew he was going through a lot, so she respected his space. Meanwhile, he sold her father's things one by one. He couldn't bring himself to stop, even when he had more than enough money to buy Dom things that would make her swoon. All he had to believe was that he was doing it for her, for Beth, and for her, for Dom. That was all the justification he needed.

Until one morning, while he was moving bins, stacking full on top of empty, and he stacked them a little off-center. They were top-heavy, and he was distracted. He was sitting on the bed responding to emails from potential buyers. He was not paying attention to the little dog that was sneaking along the base of the bed, trying not to be alone while his person was out on her run. It was true, Adam and Goliath were not best friends, but they had learned to appreciate each other's company. Goliath didn't mind one more lap to sit in or being let outside more often to patrol, so he tolerated Adam's continued presence, and even sought him out when he was lonely, or cold, or bored. However, Chihuahuas are generally skittish creatures, and when Adam swung his leg over the edge of the bed to get up and go to the bathroom, Goliath skittered backward, not looking at what he might be running into. When he hit the bottom bin, the whole tower shook. The full bin at the top of the pile made of forward jerk and tumbled down. Adam was not as alert or as agile as Beth had been at the orchard. He didn't catch it, and the bin full of electronics that had been perched up above came down hard on Goliath's back end, crushing his tiny legs under its weight.

He squealed in pain. He tried to wriggle out from under it, but it was no use. The damage had been done. Adam watched it happen and couldn't change it, couldn't fix it. There was instant remorse. It was all his fault. His pilfering had not helped her. Instead, it had hurt the one soul that was totally devoted to her. She would never forgive him.

Chapter 15

You must rip off the Band-aid for the truth to breathe.

Beth was sitting at the kitchen table with Kendra, Jackson, and Danny playing Sorry!. She had been sent back to the start at least ten times, but Danny's giggles each time made it seem like a win rather than a failure.

"Sorry, Aunt Beth!" she squealed between fits of hilarity.

"I didn't know she could be so ruthless," Jackson whispered, his speech getting softer and more difficult by the day.

"No need to worry; she's just enjoying her win. Who doesn't enjoy beating the grown-ups at that age? I remember my parents letting me win at chess a few times, and I thought I was the queen of all I surveyed," Beth said.

"Wait, are you letting me win?" Danny's giggle had turned into an adorable little scowl.

"Of course not, honey, you are winning fair and square," Jackson reassured her.

"Would anyone like some more snacks?" Kendra asked, standing at the kitchen window with a view of the front yard. "Wait, who is that in the Jeep? He's driving way too fast for a road that doesn't go anywhere!"

It was Adam, flying into the driveway like the rules didn't apply to him. It was a miracle he didn't crush Danny's bike tire that was half in the grass and half on the driveway. Beth ran out to meet him.

"What's wrong? Is everything okay?"

"No. The pile of bins in my room fell and crushed Goliath underneath them. He needs to get to the vet, like, now."

"Okay, let's go," she replied with no hesitation, nodding to Kendra as she ran to the car. She scooped up Goliath whose back half was wrapped in a towel and held him gently on her lap, crying softly and stroking his head. "Turn left at the intersection." She gave directions to Adam as he drove as fast as the law would allow, straight to the vet's office. "This is all my fault!" Beth wailed as the seriousness of the situation began to sink in.

"What do you mean? This is all my fault," Adam admitted.

"All my stuff. I knew it wasn't safe for him. I knew he deserved better."

"He was just fine until I showed up. I'm toxic. You should have left me in the street at the parade."

"Are you kidding? You've been nothing but a blessing to me, to us both."

"You won't think so when I tell you the truth."

*   *   *

While Goliath went through a long and complicated surgery, Adam explained it all. He couldn't believe what he had done as he said it out loud. The violation of her trust alone, well, it was disgusting, and he had justified it all as if he was doing her a favor. Even worse. He had bought Dominique a platinum ring with a diamond so big she would only have to look at it to see her value in his eyes.

When he finished explaining, Beth sat quietly for a long time. She didn't want to believe it, but here it was, from the horse's mouth. She thought about her dog in there fighting for his life. She thought about the man next to her, fighting for his marriage. She thought about his wife, fighting for her self-worth. She thought about her friend at her kitchen table, fighting to keep her family safe and together. Her father's things had been precious to her. The smell of his cigars had been one of the smells that tied her childhood to her present. But right now, she didn't want to fight. She didn't want to push away someone who had helped her grow, someone who still, even with this new knowledge, she felt she could trust.

As the minutes ticked by, Adam had no idea what would happen next. He wrung his hands, panicked about Goliath's condition, his friend's response, his own guilt.

"You should keep the ring," Beth said finally. "And whatever else you bought her. Everyone deserves to have the things that give them joy. Whether they are old or new, cheap or expensive, the things we curate, that we surround ourselves with, while not as important as relationships, are reflections of how we see ourselves and the world. They help us build the life we want. You did help. I don't know that I would have ever gotten rid of those sentimental things of my father's on my own. Maybe you and Dom are the ones I was supposed to help with those bins. Maybe this is how it was supposed to go. At any rate, this thing with Goliath, this is my doing."

"You...I don't know what to say."

"Don't say anything. Let's just send Goliath all the good vibes we can from here." She tipped her head back over the top of the chair and closed her eyes. He could see her lips moving, but no sound escaped. She was talking to herself, or her dog, or her dad. None of whom would ever be able to respond in the way she wanted, but that didn't stop her from sending out whatever message it was. Adam leaned back too. He breathed the relief of someone pardoned for a serious crime. The kind of crime that destroys relationships and leaves people alone in the world.

Chapter 16

"The weak can never forgive. Forgiveness is the attribute of the

strong."

– Mahatma Gandhi

Back at Moira's for the last week before the holiday break, Adam sat toasty in front of the fire with Moira, sipping hot cocoa. The snow was falling outside in slow, fat flakes. It had been a while since they'd had a white Christmas, and everything looked like a postcard. The two of them had spent many evenings like this, getting to know each other, sharing secrets. Tonight, despite the beauty of the evening, and the crackle of the fire, there was tension in the air. They made small talk, refilled mugs, sat in silence for long minutes. Then, a knock at the door.

"Come in!" Moira yelled from her chair.

Dominique bustled in, shaking the snow off her coat onto the entryway rug and removing her boots by the door. Adam got up and went to hang up her coat. He hugged her. She didn't resist. They settled themselves by the fire,

Dominique putting her feet with their woolen knitted socks up on the hearth to warm them.

Adam began to say what he'd prepared, "Dom, we need to talk."

She took her feet down and leaned toward him, "So we're getting right to it, then. No lead in?"

"We can dance around it for a while if you want, but I think you're going to want to hear what we have to say."

"We? Isn't this just about you and me?"

"No. It's not." He reached over and squeezed Moira's hand.

"Dom, I know where you came from. I know about the alley, the dumpster, the little blanket. He picked up the quilt he had found in the closet of his room and set it on his lap. To be honest, I'm a little hurt that you never shared any of it with me, but I see why you kept it to yourself. I do." Dominique looked at the blanket on his lap, puzzled. She shook her head, put her face in her hands.

"I didn't want you, or anyone, to pity me."

"I get that, really, but don't you think I could have helped you? I am a counselor, for God's sake, I am equipped."

"I didn't want a counselor. I wanted a husband. Someone who didn't know that I was trash. Someone who—"

"You are not trash!" Moira yelled with an intensity that startled all three of them.

"Excuse me, but you've met me once. You can't know how disposable I am."

Here we go, Moira thought, then said, "Dominique, Adam found an article about your adoption that I had saved and was in a drawer in his guest room upstairs. He also found the blanket that is sitting on his lap in the closet." Dominique stared hard at the blanket, put her hand over her mouth, stayed silent. "He recognized it because it was just like the one you had saved from your infancy." There was a long pause. "I made two."

Waves of sadness, then anger rolled across Dominique's face as she tried to process this information, like clouds across the sun on a windy day. She got up, started pacing behind their chairs, face squeezed between her palms.

Moira went on, twisting the tassels of the old, knitted throw blanket between her soft fingers, "I've been keeping my distance, but keeping track of all you do your whole life. I've slipped into the back of choir concerts, swim meets, even watched your wedding from my car in the parking lot at the state park. I need you to know; I wasn't throwing you away. This is such a small town. I was so young. I couldn't be seen with you. Before you were born, I worked in the summers for the Whittinghams. They were the kindest, most genuine people I ever met. I knew they had never had children but wanted to. I knew that Anne went out into the alley every morning to throw out the trash from the day before. I knew she would see you at the top of the steps. You'd be safe there until she could rescue you. She would love you. I quilted those quilts in my room at night while I was pregnant. One was for you, and one was for me. It comforted me so many nights, knowing that you had one to keep you warm too. I was never going to tell you. But Adam and I were talking, and it seemed like you needed to know. That maybe I shouldn't stay in the shadows anymore. That the story you had built in your head needed to be rewritten, softened. You weren't thrown away. You were salvaged."

Dominique couldn't help but picture her mother, Anne, sanding that old window frame, making it into a picture frame, giving it new life in the midst of old things. And here was her mother, Moira, in the midst of old things she had treasured for decades, repairing, polishing, dusting them. She made them shine for the company that longed for the good old days when Keurigs were kettles, and everyone had time to sit down for breakfast together and eat eggs gathered from the backyard. She was doubly loved.

"I don't know how to process any of this," Dominique said, shaking her head to acclimate herself. She looked from the face of her mother to the face of her husband. She had lived her whole life thinking she wasn't worthy, trying to cover herself in beautiful things so that no one would see her. The façade was cracking, but it wasn't pity that she saw in their eyes, it was regret and love.

"I'm sorry," Moira and Adam said in one voice.

Chapter 17

We will never be as great or as terrible as we fear.

Beth's run that morning was jubilant. She felt light and fast. In less than twenty minutes, she made it to Kendra's house and continued to hop as she waited on the front steps for her to come out. She had brought over the bins of toys earlier in the week, and Danny had loved them all. They even had a tea party at the kitchen table with real tea and sugar cubes. Beth hadn't put any in her pocket to bring home. She was defeating the past. She was starting a new life with people and purpose and room to move.

Kendra's face appeared at the door, tear-stained and exhausted. She was still in her pajamas, and they hung on her like she wasn't even there. She didn't look like she had the vitality to run a step. She pushed open the screen door and hugged Beth fiercely.

"Are they okay? Danny and Jackson, are they okay?"

"He must have stopped breathing last night. When I woke up to check on him, he was already gone. The ambulance is on its way. I haven't woken Danny yet. I won't know what to say to her. How will this ever be okay?"

"Oh, Kendra!" There was a long expanse of empty air. She pictured Danny's face, tasted shared ice cream, heard Loggins and Messina. "It won't be the same." They heard sirens in the distance. "Do you want me to stay? Help you manage things?"

"No, that's okay. I think we have to face this one on our own. I'll call you soon, I promise."

As Beth ran out of the cul-du-sac, she looked back at her favorite house. Now that she'd been inside, it hadn't lost any of its magic. She loved everyone even more than she had when they were just a perfect idea in her head. The lights on top of the police cruisers and ambulances were blinding in the early morning gloom, and she stopped and put her hand up to her eyes to watch them pass. She said a prayer for the woman and the girl inside that house. Two people who had given her so much, brought her back from the edge. Given her the faith to trust in people and life again. They were going to need her. She would be their rock. As she ran, she composed a short note in her head: *Kendra, It won't be the same. But someday, it may be okay. I can't predict the future, of course, but I will be here for you through it. I have been through loss. I know it's a dark tunnel, but I also know there's light at the end of it. You and Danny have been so much of the light for me. I can only*

*hope to pay it back ten-fold, to cover you with the love you've
shown me. -B*

She ran toward home, slowly. A couple blocks from
her house was a Dunkin Donuts. She went inside, ordered a
coffee and a Free Press. The aroma brought tears to her
eyes. She could barely see the crossword puzzle clues through
her watery eyes. *#1 man. A four-letter word for #1
man. Hero? No, that didn't fit the letters. Adam.* He would
be there this evening. She had made little progress throughout
the week; her work schedule had been tight. She should get
home and tidy up before work.

As she walked in the door, she set the paper on the table,
the crossword could wait for later, and headed for the shower
but was interrupted by the sound of her phone ringing in her
arm band. Maybe it was Kendra.

"Hello?" she asked, not accustomed to calls at all,
much less this early in the morning.

"Hello." Adam's deep voice cracked a little as he said
it, and he cleared his throat. "Beth, I won't be coming down
this weekend. I'm so sorry. Dominique and I have gotten
together to talk. We are going to stay at Moira's and try to work
some things out. I don't mean to desert you; I just really need
to get myself together. There is new information that I need to
consider. We have gone to full disclosure. She is--"

"It's okay," Beth said, trying to sound convincing. "That will give me more time to work on myself and the house before you come back, if you do. I hope it works out for you. I--"

"This isn't the end of our friendship, I hope. I just need to get back on my feet. Rebuild."

"Me too. Next time I see you, I bet the house will be all cleaned out. I am going to get there. I appreciate your help." She was starting to cry again; Goliath was looking up at her, eager to go out. "I have to get ready for work. Talk to you later." She hung up.

She let Goliath out, carried him down the stairs, waited. The brace on his back haunches made his patrolling more time-consuming. It was a miracle he was moving around at all. The vet said he'd been very lucky that he hadn't sustained any injuries to his vital organs. She was so grateful that her piles hadn't taken him away. He came back into the house, wagging gently but happily, a bottle of peppermint schnapps between his teeth. He dropped it into the box. Beth looked out through the screens, trying to see whoever kept littering their little bottles in her yard. This was early for them to be here. There were no cars, but she saw a man trudging away from the house down the sidewalk, head hung down, so his chin rested on his chest. His pants were too big, so he walked on the back of them, *just this side of slovenly.* He looked so sad; she couldn't call him out for dropping the bottle. Maybe the two of them weren't that different anyway; maybe he was just done keeping up appearances.

The shower beat down hot rain on her face as she sobbed for the first time since she told Kendra her story. She was mourning Jackson, and Adam, and maybe even Tony, though she didn't know his name or his story. She cried for the little girl with the beautiful tea set that would probably always remind her of the last tea party with her dad. She cried for the little girl with only one red patent leather shoe. She cried for the girl, now a woman, that had been left by that antique store dumpster. She cried hardest for the little girl on the side of the highway with her mother, laughing because they'd just cheated death. She wished life was easier. She wished she didn't have to see that big pink unicorn every day and wonder what if. She wished her parents had handled everything differently or that she had. She wondered if, as she grew, Danny would remember the octopus in her bathtub. She wanted to be there to find out.

Epilogue

"I have not broken your heart - you have broken it; and in breaking

it, you have broken mine."

- Emily Brontë *Wuthering Heights*

The holidays were hard all around. Beth spent most of her time at Kendra's. They opened presents and baked cookies, and she never thought about what the people outside would think of the lights strung haphazardly across the front of the house, drooping on the edge of the gutters. The crooked tree with its handmade ornaments, Dixie cup bells and reindeer made out of clothespins, googly eyes lolling in different directions, the snowman in the front yard whose carrot had fallen to his feet during a brief thaw. They had cried and laughed together, stirring their hot chocolate with candy canes, cuddled under blankets watching *It's a Wonderful Life*.

But now it was spring. They had started to roll down their car windows when they drove, as Beth did every day, to get rid of the clutter in her house. Her daily bin was loaded into and out of the Beetle's back seat, slowly and methodically cleaning out each room so that she and Goliath could reclaim it. Every day opened up wider aisles to walk down, more carpets to clean. Each bin removed left more open space for Goliath, who had started trying to run in his new, crooked sideways shuffle, adorable and heartwarming to watch. The cleaning continued. The progress was painstaking. She was a woman on a mission, though, not slowed by Adam's absence, or the lack of pressure to prepare things for him. Bin by bin, she had figured out how to get it done, her way, on her own steam.

In April, she invited Kendra and Danny over for the afternoon. They were going to have a polo match followed by a tea party. When they arrived on their bikes, Beth pushed the button to raise up the garage door, and Kendra gasped.

"Beth, you did it! Oh my gosh, I'm so proud of you!" She threw her arms around her friend. It felt warm and real. The garage had been the last bastion of accumulation. Truthfully, it would have been easy to overlook it since there was no longer any need to park her car inside since the snow was gone, and it wasn't staring her in the face every day when she got up. But she had wanted to be thorough. She had wanted to feel free of it all.

The cement floors were clear of any boxes and swept clean. On a hook on the wall, she took down her father's golf clubs. She didn't play but knew that they would come in handy for polo. She rolled out her bike, and they started, on the driveway and front lawn, to hit an old volleyball back and forth into the goals that were marked out with sticks Goliath had found at the park, chasing but not catching fat, happy squirrels. The ball didn't roll all that well, since the grass had been allowed to grow all week. Beth had been busy with other things.

Her house was completely clean, free of clutter, not a bin to be seen. It was a picture of minimalism, really. The carpets had all been ripped up and the floors' original hardwoods polished to a bright shine. Only essential furniture was allowed to remain. There was a picture on the wall, a portrait of her family from when Beth was five or six. It could be seen from the two chairs set up facing toward the windows, blinds and curtains removed, naked and exposed to the neighborhood. It was bright and fresh. Danny loved to run and slide across the floor in her socks. A small chandelier had replaced the ceiling fan. An area rug lay under the chairs and in the middle of it was an ottoman with a tray in the middle. On the tray was a silver tea set. The first one. The one that had started it all.

*   *   *

Adam and Dominique had sticks from their backyard too, they gathered them from around the base of their tree in which resided a plump squirrel looking down at them. They bent down in the grass, right below where their balcony had been, and wrote their initials in the fresh cement of half-circle steps that would lead to their new front door. They put a slash between them and stood up to look -- AC/DC. They laughed out loud. Adam played air guitar. Their new foundation looked strong, rock star solid. He stepped back and knelt in the grass of their houseless yard, held out the ring that he had always wanted to give her, the one he always wanted her to have. She knelt in front of him as he put it on her finger. They would start again, with all the cards on the table. They walked back to Moira's, Dominique's designer shoes clicking on the cracked sidewalks, swinging their held hands.

*   *   *

That Saturday, Adam and Beth sat at the Beantown counter, sipping lattes and doing the crossword. "How are the new house plans coming?" Beth asked, hoping he had pictures of the drawings on his phone.

"Slow, but it's fun to plan every detail. Dom and I have agreed on everything so far, except the den. I want it to feel like a dark library. She wants it to be open to the living area, bright and airy, modern. I think I like a little darkness, overstuffed furniture, hunter green, leather, and worn bindings. It feels cozy, like a womb or a tomb."

"I get it. And surrounded by all those stories, you'd never be alone."

"Exactly."

"I'm sure you'll find a compromise. There's always a way to get what you want."

"Maybe I'll build her a modern she-shed in the backyard."

"Maybe you should think about that before you suggest it." They laughed, took their books over to the fluffy couches. Feet up on the coffee table, it felt like they had found it, the balance they were looking for. The communion of two people who understood each other, forgave each other, and helped each other through it. This was the other side.

*   *   *

There was lamp glowing in storage unit 149 at the U-Store-It-All. The extension cord ran across bin after bin, all labeled and stacked neatly from the floor to as high as she could reach without a ladder, all the way to the plug by the door. In the middle of it all, in the circle of light, was an old couch, a sheet and blanket pitifully covering its worn cushions, *just this side of slovenly*. She was stretched out on it, her heels up on the arm. She was reading Adam's copy of *Anna Karenina* again. Next to her on the floor was the giant pink sparkly unicorn. She reached her hand out and patted its head as if it was Goliath. He would have loved it here, but on nights she stayed here, he stayed at the house. She couldn't risk him being the victim of her piles again. She could live the life she wanted, **and** the life she had. As she drifted off to sleep, she thought, *No one had to know. No one would ever have reason to pity her.*

Acknowledgements

A special thank you to those who helped me along the way; I am forever grateful. This project has been literal decades in my head, waiting to fully become the finished product. You helped me make it happen. First, for Emily Schmalz, my fearless editor. Thank you for being a fellow writer and friend that I can trust with honest and kind feedback. For Melissa Dodge, who helped me with a plot point when I was stuck for where to go. I was listening, and I think it adds a layer to the story. For my beta readers, your tips and encouragement gave me the courage to put this out into the world: my mom and dad, my girlfriends Lauren Stroschin, Laura Malik (my veterinary consultant), Ann O'Neill (my psychology consultant), Teri Brune, Olivia Wilsey, Trisha Lowder, Michelle Jarrin, and Ruth Fazzari.